Shadow Vista

Charles Colyott
Mark Steensland

www.encyclopocalypse.com

*To Sadie & Ashley, whose enthusiasm and support
truly proves that a high tide lifts all boats.*

-1-

"COMING SOON!" the sign said. "Luxury single family dwellings!" But the once-bright colors of this enthusiastically optimistic promise had faded and turned to rust along the edges. Not surprisingly, the model homes below the sign had suffered the same fate. What had once felt welcoming, maybe even cozy, was now little more than a collection of dark corners surrounded by chain link fence topped with razor wire and covered in cobwebs. The signs here held promises, too, printed in blood-red ink and mounted every ten feet: "WARNING! This area is under 24-hour surveillance. Trespassers will be prosecuted."

Bored teens occasionally dug their way under, on a mission to christen one of the houses, leaving behind the stale stink of gutter weed, empty beer cans, and the occasional used condom. Because many of the houses had not been finished when the subdivision ran out of money, the trespassing teens had ample choices. The new buyer, if one could be found, would have lots of reasons to wonder where the security guards had been.

No teens this night, though.

The light which shone dimly from a hooded lantern in the backyard of a house on Katz Parkway belonged to a figure dressed in heavy gray overalls, black leather gloves, and a red ski mask, now sliding a shovel from the back of a white van parked in the driveway, returning to the lantern, and beginning to dig.

Steadily.

Quietly.

Once the size of the hole met with the digger's approval, they dropped the shovel and took a utility knife from a pocket in the overalls. The blade flashed as it sliced open a large bag of concrete. Like smoke, the cement powder rose into the air as the digger dumped it into a wheelbarrow. The lantern light broke into shafts around the digger as they added water from plastic jugs and stirred the mixture with the shovel while checking the set time on the empty bag. 20 minutes wasn't a lot. But enough.

Returning to the van, the digger hauled out what looked like a carpet, wrapped tightly in plastic. The misshapen tube had been secured in several points along its length with duct tape. Using the tape like handles, the digger dead-lifted the bundle out of the back of the van, then dragged it by one end. A dark blue tennis shoe tumbled silently from the bundle, catching on the lip of the sidewalk, and tipped into the gutter, unseen.

At the edge of the freshly dug hole, the digger took the utility knife out again, extended the blade, which shone nearly white in the moonlight, and slashed open the plastic sheeting. The blade not only opened the plastic, but the fleshy cheek of the man inside, snapping him from blissful unconsciousness to wild, panicked fear in an instant. His eyes rolled nonsensically in his head, so wide that they looked like they might break free and roll away.

Smiling, the digger drew the utility razor down the man's other cheek to see if his eyes could possibly widen any farther.

Not really, it turned out.

The digger sighed with disappointment. Then, from the ground near the lantern, they picked up a small pillow—the kind of thing a traveler would pack for a long flight—and placed it carefully in the hole. With considerably less care, the digger shoved the bound man into the hole with one booted foot.

The man was trying to scream, that much was obvious from the veins standing out on his forehead and the bulging cords in his throat. There was a rubber ball gag in his mouth, though, and, on top of that, a silvery rectangle of duct tape. He barely made any sound at all.

To scream—or to attempt to scream—that part was exhausting, clearly, and after half a minute, the man was pitifully trying to suck as much air as possible through his nose (and blowing snot bubbles in the process).

Crouching beside him, the digger patted the man's cheek gently with leather-clad fingers, then picked up a trowel from the nearby tool box, dipped it into the concrete, and smeared a thick, gray X over each of the man's eyes. Before the man could blink the grit away, the digger swiped a load of cement into the man's nostrils. He blew and blew, trying to clear his air passages, but the mix really was thickening very fast.

While the man was thrashing, the digger took a moment to add a bit more water to the wheelbarrow. The man was still flopping like a fish when the digger began to pour concrete over the man's feet and legs, stopping occasionally to smooth it with the shovel. There was a high whistling coming from the man then, the concrete making his final breaths sing. The digger admired the sound for a moment, then dropped a shovelful of concrete over the man's face, silencing him forever.

Another few minutes of filling and smoothing, and the new grave looked only like another part of the patio.

Flicking off the lantern, the shadows rolled in like nothing had happened there at all.

- 2 -

Zachary Frenkel pulled onto the freeway, the windows of his Camry vibrating from the bass on his stereo. The song was "Somebody to Love" by Jefferson Airplane, an odd choice for a twenty-something white kid from the suburbs, maybe, but classic rock had always been his jam. He had grown up with his mother's awesome vinyl collection. Originals of Airplane, the Beatles, Jimi, you name it. Their stupid-ass cats had destroyed the sleeves over time, using the stack of albums as a makeshift scratching post. The music stuck, though, becoming a part of him. And so, as he drove, windows vibrating, he also sang. Loudly, poorly, and out of key, but he sang, drumming his fingers on the steering wheel at the same time.

The music had put him in a good mood. Work would suck, sure, but in that same old predictable way that it always did. The greatest foe a security guard ever faced was boredom, and out at Shadow Vista, that particular foe lurked around every corner.

Glancing into the rearview mirror, he bared his teeth, checking for any stray food particles that might mar his smile. While he did so, he also caught a glimpse of his uniform. That rare blend of paramilitary and macho '80s bro. Okay, he thought, maybe that wasn't really so rare. Tin Star Security, his badge read.

Yes, indeed.

It was Zachary and his co-workers who kept the abandoned development safe from ... what? Homeless people? Stray dogs? Litter? Acid rain? Harsh language? What?

That part didn't matter. Not to Zachary, anyway. He was taking classes at the local community college in the hopes of getting a degree in criminal justice and becoming a cop. He figured a job as a security guard would look good on his resume. And Tin Star had been kind enough to hire him even though he didn't have any experience. He found out why quickly enough. The job mostly involved sitting in an office all night and messing around on Facebook.

After almost missing his exit while inspecting himself, he flashed a parental glance at his reflection in the rearview, turned the music down slightly, and paid more attention to the road. He drove past the locked gate at the entryway of the development, the empty streets beyond reminding him, as always, of sets from some old nuclear holocaust movie. Near the rear of the property sat the security trailer, and Zach eagerly drove past Bob's pickup and Kyle's Jeep so he could park next to Rebecca's Civic. He was still whistling the Jefferson Airplane song as he locked his car and ran up the ramp to the trailer, threw open the door, and entered.

"Hey, good afternoon everybody. Rebecca. Bob."

His boss, leaning back in his chair and flipping idly through a gun magazine, grunted. Rebecca smiled. It was strictly professional, but Zachary didn't notice. Mainly because the new blouse she was wearing showed more cleavage than usual. Cleavage that was far more impressive than he had dared to even imagine. And he always thought he had a great imagination.

He walked over to Rebecca's office, leaned against her desk and said, "So ... How's your day been so far?"

"You're early," she said. "Again."

He glanced at the clock. 2:33. He didn't work until 3:00. Crap. "Oh ... Yeah. I never know how traffic is going to be, y'know?"

"Don't you live like fifteen minutes from here?"

"Well, yeah," he said, "but you should see it sometimes. At rush hour it's a total nightmare."

"Oh."

God, he thought, she was perfect. Long, blonde hair. flawless skin. Big, guileless blue eyes. Long, perfectly muscled legs. Rockin' curves. She looked like the kind of girl who spent her mornings doing yoga, her afternoons hitting the CrossFit gym, and her evenings learning Taekwondo to fend off all the goons who noticed the rest of the work she'd put in.

"Why don't you use a GPS?"

He shrugged and crossed his arms. "I don't know. I've never really trusted those things."

"Tell me about it," she said and leaned forward, resting her elbows on the desk. The neckline of her top yawned, giving Zachary a glimpse of the most perfect set of breasts he'd ever seen in person. Granted, that wasn't a super high number or anything, but still. He'd seen a lot of movies, too, and this still topped it all.

Then he realized that Rebecca had caught him looking.

Shiiit.

"Hey," he said quickly, "is that a new blouse?"

She raised one eyebrow. "Yes."

"I thought so. Looks great, by the way. Where'd you find it?"

She smiled hesitantly. "Forever 21. At the mall. Why?"

"Oh," he started, then realized he hadn't really thought that far ahead. "Uh ... well, my mom's birthday is coming up..." His brain screamed for him to stop, but his mouth continued. "And I thought, 'Hey, that would look really great on her.'"

Yes, dumbass, he thought. That's exactly what your crush wants to hear. Because it either means that a) her new top looks like something your mother would wear, or b) you want to check out your mom's boobs, too.

What a fucking doucher you are.

Rebecca was still smiling, but it was a weird smile now. The kind of smile that said, "Wow, this guy's a real fuckin' doucher."

He let out a small sigh.

Suddenly Bob was there, the gun magazine in his meaty fist. "Frenkel, what did I tell you about bothering Ms. Summers?"

Zach stood awkwardly and said, "Not to."

"That's correct. And what are you currently doing?"

"B-Bothering her, I guess," Zachary said. "And I'm sorry, Mr. Brashear. I didn't realize how early I was, and we were just talking about that and I..."

"Not remotely interested, Frenkel. Get to work."

"B-But sir, it's not 3:00 yet."

"That's all right. Kyle said he thought there might be a dead rat in a driveway on Trellman. Why don't you check it out? And don't forget to grab some gloves from the supply closet. I wouldn't want you to get any liquid rat on your hands."

Zach inwardly scowled. He outwardly smiled, though. Because Bob Brashear was a big, scary son of a bitch.

"C'mon, Bob. I did rat patrol last time. Give me a break, please? I'm early."

Bob glared at him and said, "Go wait in the damned muster room, then. And don't even think about clocking in early."

"No, sir," Zachary said. He glanced at Rebecca and smiled when he saw her browser was open to her Facebook profile.

In the muster room (a plain room in the security trailer with two folding card tables pushed together into a makeshift conference table), Zachary sat and scrolled through Facebook on his phone. He leaned his chair back, onto the rear two legs, and looked through the doorway into Rebecca's office. She was pushing a strand of hair behind her ear.

Oof, he thought. Even a gesture as simple as that was sexy.

He heard a heavy sigh and saw Bob staring at him, still clutching the gun magazine like a baton. Zachary quickly dropped his chair back to all four legs, stood, and walked over to the soda machine. After taking a dollar from his wallet and feeding it carefully into the slot, he pushed the button for his selection, but nothing happened. Bob was still watching him.

Under his breath, Zachary muttered, "C'mon ... C'mon..."

With a sigh, he walked back into the entryway, ready to ask Bob (or, better yet, Rebecca) for a different bill to try on the fussy machine. Before he could, though, the front door swung open and Bob's son Kyle entered. Like his father, Kyle favored the military approach to security. The big difference, though, was that Bob had actually served. Kyle's only experience was playing Call of Duty against ten-year olds on the internet.

Kyle was stomping the dust from his army surplus boots when Rebecca said, "Kyle! How many times do I have to ask you to do that outside?"

He immediately stopped, let his eyes trace their way down Rebecca's body in a way that Zachary (and, Zachary assumed, Rebecca also) didn't like at all, and said, "Right. Sorry. I forgot, okay? But listen, I forgot for a good reason. Check this out."

He held up a dark blue tennis shoe.

"Your shoe," Rebecca said.

"Yeah. No. I mean it's a shoe. But it's not mine. I think that homeless dude is back."

Bob got up from his desk and walked over. "Let me see."

Kyle handed his father the shoe. Bob wiped the dust from it and then flipped it over to examine the sole. "Looks practically brand new. Where'd you find it?"

Shoving his hands into his pockets, Kyle said, "In the gutter on Katz. On the northwest end. Not far from that hole in the fence where he used to come in."

Bob looked at his son. "But we fixed that," he said.

"Hell, yeah. Like six months ago."

Bob looked at the shoe again. Zachary wasn't sure how much information could really be gleaned from staring at a shoe, but Bob sure seemed committed to gleaning whatever he could.

"Did you check inside any of the houses?"

"Didn't have time," Kyle said. "Figured swing shift'd do it."

The three of them turned toward Zachary.

Zachary swallowed and said, "Yeah, sure. And, uh, when you get a chance, the soda machine is still broken."

Kyle smirked at him. "No, it's not."

Walking past Zachary into the muster room, Kyle glanced back, at Zachary first, then at Rebecca, before punching the side of the soda machine. A can of Dr. Pepper immediately clattered into the delivery tray.

"Told you," Kyle said with a grin.

Getting up to retrieve his soda, Zachary said, "Thanks, but if you have to resort to violence, I'd say it's broken."

Zachary opened his soda, quickly putting his mouth over the lip of the can to catch the foam as it spilled out. Kyle pointedly ignored him. Rebecca finished shutting down her computer and stood. She picked up her purse and fished for her keys. Bob glanced at the clock on the wall, dropped his gun mag on his desk, and sighed.

Rebecca squeezed past Kyle to the door and, glancing at Zachary as she walked by, smiled. Zachary was too paralyzed by shock and hormones to smile back immediately, and by the time his face caught up, she had already looked away.

Still, he thought, that was some sort of progress, right?

Kyle pushed past Zachary to walk behind Rebecca, and his motives were crystal clear. He was shamelessly staring at her as she walked out.

- 4 -

Soda in hand, Zachary followed them. He stood at the top of the steps and watched Rebecca climb into her silver Civic. Bob nearly knocked him off the step as he made his way down to his truck. No malice in it, Bob was a big dude who'd only gotten bigger over the years, and he'd never quite understood how big.

Kyle was still openly ogling Rebecca when he straightened abruptly and faced his father. "Oh! Almost forgot. The truck's about out of gas."

Bob grumbled under his breath, dug his wallet from his pocket, and pulled out a $100 bill. Handing it to Zachary, he said, "Use what you need to fill it up, then put the change and the receipt in the envelope on Rebecca's desk." To Kyle, he added, "Did you remember to leave the keys?"

Kyle frowned and felt his pockets. Clearing his throat, he pulled the set of truck keys from his pocket and tossed them to Zachary, who fumbled them a little but still caught them. "Sorry," Kyle said. "That was a close one. Good thing I remembered."

Zachary nodded and shrugged. Bob's irritation was palpable.

From what Zachary could tell, the old man really did love his son, but he was fully aware of what Kyle was: a world class poser and wannabe.

Zachary sort of always imagined that this job was intended to toughen Kyle up, to "make a man out of him," but he wasn't entirely sure how. Shadow Vista was a snooze zone. The job was the easiest one Zachary had ever had, and he'd once been a greeter in Walmart's blue vest brigade.

"See you at home?" Kyle said as he climbed into his Jeep.

Bob nodded and watched as his son backed out of the parking lot and drove away. Maybe it was Zachary's imagination, but he liked to think that he could actually feel the waves of dis-appointment flowing from the old man. Mainly because he, Zachary, thought Kyle was kind of a dickhead.

Turning back to Zachary, Bob said, "Keep an eye out for that homeless guy. And don't let Sam talk you into doing nothing but escorting him off property like she did with Ollie. I want you to call the cops if you see anybody messing around, got it?"

"Yes, sir."

A refurbished 1969 yellow Volkswagen Beetle back-fired and both of them turned to see what had made the sound. "Speak of the devil," Bob said.

As the Beetle parked, the door opened and Zachary's partner for the night, Samantha Wong, got out. She ran a hand through her short dark hair and grinned at them. "Hey there, fellas," she said.

"Cutting it a bit close, aren't you?" Bob said.

"I'm not late."

Bob glanced at his watch.

"What? I'm not!"

Bob shrugged. "Y'all have a good shift."

"We shall remain ever vigilant," Sam said, nodding.

Bob drove off, and Sam climbed the steps to join Zachary. After a moment, she said, "Jughead forgot to fill the tank again."

"How the hell did you know that?"

"Fantastic," Sam said, pushing past him to get to the door.

"Seriously," he said. "How do you do that?"

"Do what?"

"Guessing that he hadn't filled the tank."

"I'm a master detective."

She turned and went into the trailer. Zachary followed. "Are you going to actually tell me or what?"

"It's about paying attention. Which is kind of the job."

"Okay..."

She laughed and adjusted her chunky-framed glasses. "Zach. You're holding the keys and a crisp $100 bill. Given what we know about Kyle, what else could it be?"

Zachary frowned and looked down at his hand. Sure enough, there they were: keys and cash.

"Oh. Well, still. I'm not sure I would've noticed."

"And you want to be a cop?"

"Well ... maybe, yeah..."

"Need to start paying attention, son."

"C'mon! How do you do it?"

"I'm observant. Always have been."

"You're more than that."

She turned toward him dramatically, cocking her head and batting her eyelashes. "Oh, Zachary, do you really think so?"

He rolled his eyes at her and said, "C'mon, you know

what I mean. Okay, yes, this time it was pretty obvious, I guess, but you've pulled some downright Sherlockian shit before."

"It's true. I'm a badass." She slipped her duty belt on and checked each item as she secured it in place: Taser, tonfa, radio, and pepper spray.

Zachary groaned in frustration.

"Okay, listen. It's not magic. It's about being present, and it's about paying attention. Seeing what's right in front of you. That's all. Maybe it takes some practice, I dunno. It's kind of how I've always operated. Just pay attention. It's super obvious when you do." She checked her flashlight, jiggled it to make sure the battery connection was good. "Like with you and Rebecca."

Zachary snorted. "What's that supposed to mean?"

Sam giggled. "Okay, if you do become a cop, don't go under-cover because you are, hands down, the worst liar I've ever met."

Zachary felt himself blush. "What about me and Rebecca?"

"You're so obvious. It's kinda painful to watch."

Zachary crossed his arms tightly without noticing he'd done so and said, "About what, exactly?"

"About everything, dude. You're like a little puppy running around after her, tongue wagging, drool spilling. And let me give you a pro tip, bro: chicks might love puppies because they think they're adorable, but they aren't turned on by them."

"How would you know?"

Sam looked at him over the top of her glasses and said, "Are you seriously so unobservant you never noticed I'm a girl?"

Zachary uncrossed his arms and stuttered, "Of course I noticed, but..."

"But what? Oh, I'm not a girl like Rebecca, so how could I possibly know what the goddess of beauty thinks?"

Zachary stammered again, "I ... I never said that."

Sam's face crinkled. "To tell you the truth? I bet she's gay."

"But she's had boyfriends."

Sam wasn't impressed. "And I've had girlfriends. Doesn't mean that's the way I am. You know what a beard is?"

Zachary frowned. "Course I know what a beard is."

Sam stared at him for a minute, eyes narrowed, and a smile on her face that he didn't like. "Nah, you don't know. C'mon. Let's get the truck gassed up. I'm ready to straight up murder some donuts."

Sam held out her hand, palm up, and waited. Zachary realized suddenly that she wanted the keys, and he handed them over. The entire conversation left him feeling strangely uncomfortable, but he wasn't sure why. He supposed it was the experience of Sam seeing right through him that left him rattled. She really would be a great cop. Perps would melt under her questioning.

5

As Zachary finished filling the tank, he caught himself staring at the Tin Star Security decal on the side of the truck. It was sun-faded and peeling at one edge. Air bubbles rippled one edge. Much like the rest of Shadow Vista, it looked tacky. Shoddy.

After returning the pump to its cradle, he glanced over and saw Sam through the mini-mart window. She was still choosing donuts. While so many people that he knew were on some variation of a low-carb diet, Sam Wong seemed to subsist solely on carbs, the simpler the better.

And he had to admit that it was working for her. She was smaller than him, both in height and weight, but she still had a solid build. Sturdy. And while she was nothing at all like Rebecca, he had to admit that there was something distinctly appealing about Sam. He'd really only ever seen her in the stupid boxy security uniforms that they both wore, but there was still something there. Something in the way she moved, maybe.

She glanced up, saw him staring at her, and raised an eyebrow.

Panicking, he waved, stupidly, and grabbed the squeegee from its murky bucket and began furiously cleaning the windshield.

A few minutes later she joined him and handed over the change with a laugh. Stopping, Zachary slumped. "What now? Am I doing it wrong or something?"

Sam threw her box of donuts into the truck and faced him. "No, you're doing fine. But you're too nice."

Zachary started to protest, but she raised her hands and said, "Listen, nice is great for a girl like me. I like nice guys. Girls like Rebecca?" She shook her head sadly.

Zachary threw the squeegee back into the bucket and threw away his paper towels. As they drove back to Shadow Vista, he said, "Are you saying I'm not supposed to be nice?"

Sam shook her head and said, "That's not what I meant. Girls like Rebecca want a manly man. And something a manly man would never do is clean another man's windshield. Look at Kyle. He treated you like his bitch today, and there you are making the truck all nicey-nice for him."

"I was making it 'nicey-nice' for you. Windshield was dusty."

"That's sweet of you, but still. Keep that shit up, you may as well give Bob a foot massage or something."

Zach slumped slightly in his seat.

"You can clean my VW's windows any time, though."

"Gee, thanks."

They drove in silence for several minutes before Sam said, "You want my advice?"

"Not really."

"Forget her and find a girl who likes you for you, y'know?"

They pulled up to the gate, and Zachary hopped out of

the truck to unlock it. He waited while Sam pulled through and then locked it again.

When he climbed back into the truck, he said, "Oh, I forgot to tell you. Kyle found a shoe. Bob thinks that homeless guy is back."

Sam nodded and said, "Probably. Forecast says we've got a rainy weekend ahead."

"Bob wants us to check the houses. Do a thorough sweep. Said we're supposed to call the cops this time if we find him."

Sam snorted derisively. "We're not calling the cops on that dude. He's not hurting anything. Just looking for a place to sleep."

"And shit, in case you forgot."

Sam busted out laughing. "Oh, shit, I did forget about that."

"It's not funny," Zachary said.

"Yes it is! This goes back to your powers of observation. Like, I could almost understand if it was dog shit or something, but the sheer size of that thing..."

"Sam, c'mon!"

"Did you ever get those boots clean?"

Zach cleared his throat and quietly said, "I threw them out."

This only made Sam laugh harder.

6

The northwest corner of the subdivision was the least developed. When funding fell through and construction had stopped, this area only had future plots sectioned off, sidewalks poured, and the occasional basement dug out. Mostly, though, it was bare dirt.

The two security officers emerged from the truck and walked across the abandoned yards to the edge of the property. Sam crouched down to inspect the chain link.

"Did you see the repair job Kyle did?" Sam asked, strumming the fence like a guitar, making it jangle. "Look at this stunning piece of crapsmanship."

Zachary hadn't ever taken the time to check the fence. The area wasn't visible from the road, as a pile of fill dirt blocked that corner. Here, though, he could see that where the fence had been clipped open with wire cutters, Kyle had laid a spare piece of chain link over the damaged section and clumsily wired it into place with zip ties and bits of spare wire.

He also noticed that the ground was littered with several crushed soda cans, twists of wire, and other trash.

Seeming to read Zachary's mind, Sam added, "He's a litter-bug, too. Where did he say he found the shoe?"

"In a gutter on Katz. Close to this end."

Sam stood, scanned the ground and the surrounding area, and said, "C'mon. Let's take a look around."

They walked back to the truck in silence. He'd learned not to interrupt her when she was in the zone like this. Instead, he watched her work. She seemed to be absorbing data from the environment like a robot. Zachary tried to follow her gaze, but whatever she was seeing, he only saw dirt.

Together, they got into the truck again and drove slowly along Katz Parkway. They passed empty slabs, then a half-dozen houses that had been mostly framed. When they reached a section of nearly completed homes, Sam slowed down and pulled over.

Zachary looked at her. "Why are we stopping here?"

"Because," Sam said, and pointed through the wind-shield at the muddy tire tracks in the driveway of the house marked 7237.

Now that she pointed them out, they were as clear as if someone had spray-painted graffiti on the ground, but Zachary had to admit to himself that he hadn't noticed before.

"Kyle must've parked there when he spotted the shoe."

Zachary nodded, as if that was what he'd been thinking, too.

"Let's check it out," Sam said, and Zachary nodded again.

As they approached the front door, Sam gestured that they should split up. She would go to the right, he would go left, and they'd meet up in the back. They were checking to make sure that no one had broken any windows, including the basement windows, and slipped inside the house somehow. That turned out not to be a problem, though, so they walked together back to the front door. Sam entered the code into the lockbox—7237—and took the keys from it to open the door.

Inside, the air was thick, stale, and humid. Dust motes floated on the slight breeze they carried with them, otherwise the interior was still, stuffy.

The walls were drywall, taped but not yet textured, and, without the benefit of lights, the interior was more than a little spooky. Zachary found himself thinking about some of the horror movies he'd seen back in junior high. The kinds of movies with half-naked girls being chased by inbred cannibals or slashers or something. And he abruptly realized something else: he wasn't sure he knew the difference between a vacant property that was still and quiet because it was long empty, and the kind of supposedly vacant property that had inbred cannibals lying in wait, ready to jump out and carve up unsuspecting, unqualified security guards with a chainsaw.

"Hello?"

Zachary jumped, startled badly, and grabbed at his chest.

Sam continued, "Anybody here?" Then, she grinned at Zachary and said, "Sorry. Did I scare you?"

"Of course not. I thought I saw something over there, and..."

She looked at him with an expression of amusement.

"Never mind," he said.

She chuckled softly and flipped on her flashlight.

Turning the corner into the kitchen, she quickly tapped him on the shoulder and gestured with the beam of the flashlight.

There was an open packet of Oreos on the kitchen counter.

She looked at him, and any trace of playfulness was gone now. Someone had been here, or maybe still was. Was there some method of entry that they'd missed?

Moving through the kitchen into the hallway, Zachary was momentarily disoriented by the abrupt shift from the unfinished front of the house to the nearly finished rear half. They had stepped from concrete slab into carpeted hallway. And from where they stood, they could see three open doors—leading, if Zachary remembered the floorplan of this model correctly, to two bedrooms and a half bath. The door at the far end was closed.

Moving swiftly down the hall, the two of them each did a sweep of the bedroom before glancing into the bath. Then, at the closed door, Zachary took the pepper spray from his belt and nodded to Sam to open the door. Sam looked at Zachary to make sure he was ready. He took a deep breath, let it out slowly and steeled himself. He nodded.

She threw the door open and he moved in and to the right, doing a quick visual sweep as Sam entered and moved left.

None of this was in their training, but, having been raised on cop shows and *Lethal Weapon* movies, it was in their DNA.

The room was empty. But it hadn't always been.

A bed sheet, like a curtain, was tacked over the window which faced the outer border of the property. A bedroll, wound tightly and secured with bright orange bungee cords, leaned against the wall in one corner.

Then Zachary noticed that the sliding closet door was open a few inches.

He moved closer to it, lifting the pepper spray can in his right hand. He opened the door quickly and raised the can to what he assumed was inbred cannibal eye level, but saw no one. At least, not at first.

The lower levels of the closet were clearly empty, other than occasional sprinkles of mouse shit. It was the sleeping bag on the upper shelf that made him pause. That's because it wasn't rolled up or folded. It bulged as if someone were in it, even though it was stuffed in at what was, at best, an uncomfortable angle. He reached up to pull the bag down and found resistance. Whatever was inside it was heavy.

Swallowing hard, Zachary found the zipper and began to pull it down. He felt the weight shift toward him and, almost simultaneously, saw a tuft of blonde hair as the bag and its contents fell toward him.

7

Zachary leapt backward, but something cold and clammy slid along his cheek as the sleeping bag fell. His mind registered it as a hand, fingers caressing his cheek, and he instantly felt nauseated.

"FUCK SHIT FUCK FUCK SHIT HOLY SHIT FUCK!" He was screaming as he jumped away from the sleeping bag. And there it was and he could actually see it now. A hand. A fucking hand. Holy fucking shit. A dead fucking body was in the sleeping bag and it fell on him and it FUCKING TOUCHED HIS FACE.

And then Sam was instantly beside him, on her knees crouching and reaching for the sleeping bag.

"DON'T TOUCH IT!" he screamed. "We have to call the cops."

She glanced at him, and there was something in her eyes that he didn't like, but he couldn't put a name on that expression. It was part fear, part ... what? Mockery?

And he had the strangest thought then: what if Sam was responsible for this? What if she'd killed some poor homeless dude and stuffed him in the bag? And as ridiculous as the thought was, his brain started to unspool the conspiracy of it all. This was how she knew exactly where to go, after all. She wasn't Sherlock Holmes. She was Hannibal Fucking Lector. And in the span of a millisecond, it all made sense. And the look on her face? That was the fear of being caught mingled with the thrill of murdering yet another poor unsuspecting bastard. Zachary tightened his grip on the can of pepper spray and was seriously considering unloading the thing into his coworker's face, but then she unzipped the sleeping bag and suddenly everything didn't make all that much sense anymore.

Because, while he was looking at a body in a sleeping bag, it wasn't a human body. At least, not a real one.

And then Sam erupted into relieved laughter.

When she could breathe again, she said, "Oh my God! Holy shit, that was terrifying for a second, huh?"

Zachary took several breaths and waited for his heart rate to return to normal. "What the hell is that? It's not a ... a mannequin..."

Sam stared at him in amazement. "You really don't know?"

Zachary looked back at the figure on the floor. Whatever it was made of, and it must've been some kind of soft rubber or plastic or something, it was definitely softer than a mannequin. It also seemed to move more or less like a real body would. It was female, blonde, and dressed in a white blouse and black skirt. There was an uncanny quality to it, very close to real looking, but clearly not. And that was what made it especially creepy.

"No," he said. "Do you?"

She stifled another laugh, then said, "Yes, I have an idea."

He got the feeling that she was struggling not to laugh at him, and he felt heat rush into his face.

"Well, what the hell is it then?"

She looked at him again and blushed a little. It was something he'd never seen her do before.

"That, Zachary, is a sex doll."

"A what?"

"Yeah. Y'know ... like a blow-up doll? Only this is one of those expensive ones. Are you seriously telling me you've never seen one of these before? Haven't you ever been on the internet?"

Zach realized he was still holding the pepper spray and felt very stupid. As he put it back into its holster on his belt, he said, "Yeah, but I ... I don't go looking for things like that..."

Sam stood and smiled at him. "If anybody else said that —and I mean ANYBODY else—I'd call bullshit. You? I believe."

"What's that supposed to mean?"

"It's a compliment."

"Doesn't sound like one."

"I literally just told you that you're voted least likely to fuck a chunk of plastic. That's a definite compliment."

Zachary was still not entirely convinced, but the trajectory of the conversation was making him uncomfortable, so he let it go.

Sam seemed to sense the shift as well, and, clearing her throat, said, "You know what this means, right?"

He looked at the doll on the floor, back at Sam, and said, "That homeless dude stole it from someone and brought it here?"

"No, dork! It's Kyle's!"

"What?"

She pointed to the bedroll in the corner. "Does that look like it's spent any time outside? No. This is Kyle's little playhouse, which explains why he takes so fucking long when he's on patrol. Oh, I'm going to vomit." Sam truly did look sickened.

Zachary thought about what she said, looked back down at the doll, and felt a bit queasy himself. "Ew," he said.

Sam nodded emphatically, stopped, and said, "Shit."

"What?"

"We've gotta put it back the way it was."

"What? Why? I'm not touching that thing."

"Dude, I don't want to either, but we can't leave it out."

"Why not, what's he going to do, bring it up at the next staff meeting? 'It has come to my attention that someone has been messing with my sex doll.' I don't think so."

Sam laughed at that, but then turned serious. "No, he wouldn't bring it up, but he'd know it was us. It could only be us. He knows David and Ollie never bother with rounds. And then he'd make sure to tell his dad to give us every shit assignment possible, or he'd set us up to get fired. You remember how he was with that guy Jake? He made his life a living hell, and I'm pretty sure that was only over a six pack of beer and not some weird sex toy stuff."

Zachary remembered exactly how Kyle had been with Jake and didn't want any part of that. "I guess you're right."

They worked together to slide the doll back into the sleeping bag. They lifted it onto the tall shelf in the closet and, after it was stowed away, Sam made sure to leave the closet door open slightly. "That's about how it was, right?"

"I think so, yeah."

Sam looked over the room, checking to make sure they hadn't missed anything. "Let's get out of here and back to someplace with a working sink. I need to scrub my hands with bleach."

"Me, too," Zachary said, trying not to think about the hand that had touched his face and how slimy it had felt.

Sam moved toward the front door and Zachary followed her.

"What about the other houses?" he asked.

"They can wait. If our homeless friend is out there, he'll probably have a fire once the sun's down and the temp drops. It'll be easier to spot him if he does."

Zachary nodded and they headed outside to the truck.

8

"You said a doll like that is expensive."

"Yeah, why? You thinking of buying one?"

He felt that heat in his face again. "No. I was curious, that's all. Wondered how much Kyle spent on something like that."

Sam stopped to unlock the driver's side of the truck and said, "Probably like six or seven hundred bucks. Maybe more. I'm not an expert or anything."

"Are you serious?"

As they both climbed in the truck, Sam said, "Oh, yeah. I'm pretty sure they have these robotic ones that cost a few grand."

"That's so fucking weird."

"I know, right? But you ain't seen nothing yet."

On the way back to the office, Sam told Zachary about things she'd seen in some documentary she'd watched on HBO late one night. Zachary wasn't a prude or anything, but there was something a little discomforting talking about weird sex stuff with your female coworker, especially when it was night and it was only the two of you. It wasn't like

Sam was flirting with him. That's not how she was. She was just so matter-of-fact about it all.

When they got back in the office, after each of them thoroughly washed their hands (and Zachary washed his face), Sam booted up Rebecca's computer and started surfing some of the seedier areas of the internet, because apparently telling Zachary about gross stuff wasn't nearly enough for her.

And so, for what felt like an eternity (but actually lasted only about 20 minutes) she showed him a wide array of horrific images that he never wanted to see. Dogs humping Thanksgiving turkeys, severed latex feet with built in vaginas, something called "blue waffle" that was neither blue nor a waffle. And with every new horror, Sam looked gleeful at Zachary's revulsion.

"I don't want to see any more," he finally said, standing and moving away from the computer.

"Aw, c'mon, you big baby. Don't you want to know what a lemon party is?"

"No, I do not."

"Well, fine. But you have to admit that Kyle doesn't seem like such a weirdo anymore, does he?"

She was staring at him, one eyebrow raised inquisitively.

He realized she was right. "No. No, I don't. And do you realize how wrong that is?"

She started laughing again.

"God, I need to shower forever."

She laughed harder, fighting to breathe.

"Just stop it, okay?"

"I can't! I can't help it. You're so cute when you're revolted."

"What?"

"You really aren't like other people, Zach. And I mean that in the best way possible."

Zachary pointed in the general direction of Rebecca's computer and said, "Are you trying to say that most people are like the ones you've been showing me?"

"In my experience? Sadly, yes."

"I don't think that's true."

"I know you don't. That's why I like you."

Zachary looked at the clock on the wall over Sam's shoulder. It was now 10:15.

"We better make our rounds."

"You sure you don't want to grab a bite to eat first?"

"That's the absolute last thing I want to do."

She grinned. "Aw, c'mon. Turkey sandwich?"

"Stop."

"Or peanut butter?"

"Sam!"

"How about a waffle?"

"Sam!!! I'm serious. I'm going to barf."

- 9 -

Zachary pushed the office door open and walked into the cool, clear night. Sam was on his tail, cheerfully saying, "I was thinking maybe we should walk. Quieter that way. Element of surprise and all that. If he hears the truck, he might put the fire out."

Zachary nodded and said, "Nice night for a walk, anyway."

Together, they headed for the main gate and went through. While Zachary locked it behind them, Sam took her flashlight from her belt.

It was quiet except for the sound of their shoes on the concrete and their breath. After several minutes, Zachary said, "I heard another developer was here last week."

"Oh, yeah?"

"I also heard Bob say that if this place does sell, he's done."

"Whattaya mean, done?"

"Like, retired."

Sam snorted. "Are you kidding me? He's already practically retired! All he does is sit in his office all day reading his precious gun magazines."

Zachary nodded. "I know, but he's still got all of us to deal with. Insurance, payroll, that sort of thing. I think his wife dealt with most of the day-to-day stuff, but now that she's gone..."

Sam's smile faded and she said, "Well, okay. Yeah, I can see that. If he did retire, closed up shop, what would you do?"

Zachary shrugged and said, "Hopefully I'll be in the academy by then."

"You really want to be a cop?"

"Why do you say it like that?"

"Like what?"

"Like it's the goofiest thing you've ever heard or something."

It was Sam's turn to shrug. "Well ... I guess because I don't really think you have the stomach for it."

"I've got a strong stomach."

"Puh-leeze. You couldn't handle it when I showed you that photo of a vajankle."

Zachary paused. "Okay," he said. "That's true."

"What are you going to do when the vajankle is made from some girl's actual, rotting, severed foot, huh?"

Zachary recoiled in disgust.

"Exactly," Sam said. "Look, you want to know what it's really like? I know a few guys. I can give them a call. See if they'll talk to you, maybe even take you on a ride-along."

"You'd do that?"

"Hell, somebody should. I mean, what's the point of fighting your way through academy training if you're going to whoops your cookies the first time you see a body or something?"

"Thanks, Sam."

"Don't mention it," she said and checked her watch. "We better split up. You go that way. Call me on the radio if you see anything, all right?"

He nodded and took his flashlight from his belt and awkwardly saluted her with it. "See you soon," he said.

Once Zachary was out of sight, Sam raced along the other side of the subdivision. Most of the homes on her side were nearly complete, and in the moonlight, they looked like looming sentries. Empty shells with yawning black eyes, the flawless concrete driveways seeming, in the darkness, like bone white tombs.

After all this time, and after a thousand rounds, Sam still had to admit that the place sometimes kind of freaked her out.

She remembered this old foreign movie she'd seen as a kid. It had been a zombie movie or something ... at least, she remembered a zombie priest in it. But outside of a scene where a girl vomited her intestines, the thing that had really freaked Sam out was something a little more subtle. There'd been a scene where someone was running through a neighborhood, and they'd been screaming for help, but even though it was a heavily populated neighborhood, and even though the homes had lights on inside, no one came to help. And that was what had stuck with her, and that memory was what freaked her out whenever she did rounds on her own like this.

She picked up the pace and, behind the fence of a house on Trellman Place, saw a flicker of light. She approached it quietly and slowly opened the gate. The flame she'd seen flickered in a small barbeque grill on the edge of the patio. A battered aluminum pan sat on the grill, though Sam couldn't see what was inside it.

An old man leapt from the shadows, eyes wide with panic, and cocked an aluminum baseball bat at his shoulder.

"Back!" he yelled. "You stay the hell back!"

Sam raised her hands. "No! Joe! It's me!" Sam shone her flashlight on her own face and Joe visibly slumped and let the baseball bat clang onto the patio.

"Don't DO that," he said. "I could've killed you!"

Looking around quickly, Sam put a finger to her lips and said, "Shh! Joe, you have to be quiet."

"Why? Is that other bastard with you?"

"No, not him. Another one."

"The cute one?" he said, wagging his bushy eyebrows.

"Be quiet and listen to me. Put that fire out. And no more fires for the next few days, okay?"

"But it's cold out, and a man has to eat."

"A man could end up in jail," she said. "Do you want that?"

"No. I'll never go back. Not ever."

"I know. That's why I need you to do what I'm telling you to do. They found one of your shoes."

Puzzled, the old man looked down at his feet and frowned. Sam followed his gaze and saw the old man's big toes wiggling through the torn leather of his tennis shoes.

"I'm not missing a shoe."

"You sure?"

The old man frowned. "Course I'm sure. Man in my position? Shoes are maybe the most important thing I own."

Sam aimed her flashlight around the yard. "You bring somebody with you, Joe?"

"No, no, no. You said I couldn't, remember? Made me promise. And I keep my promises."

"Somebody follow you, maybe?"

"No. No way. Not since the fence was fixed."

Sam studied the weathered old face. As far as she knew, Joe had never lied to her. It wasn't in him.

"All right. Just do what I say and lay extra low for the next few days. I'll bring you some more food as soon as I can, okay?"

Joe patted her shoulder and said, "Thank you, sweetie."

Sam waited for a moment. "The fire, Joe, you have to put it out. Now!"

The old man mumbled "right, right" as he carefully lifted the aluminum pan from the grill. Then, turning, he took a gallon milk jug full of water from where it sat on the ground, next to a wheelbarrow, and used the water to extinguish the flames.

Sam watched ghosts of steam rise from the hissing coals, then, satisfied the fire was out, flashed a smile and waved to Joe as she backed away from the patio and went to the gate.

When she opened it, she found herself inches away from a figure cloaked in shadow.

10

Sam screamed, but the figure raised a flashlight to their chin, illuminating the familiar face of Zachary. "Sorry," he said. "Did I scare you?" He looked amused.

Though she was immediately relieved to see it was him, she also realized that, this close to the patio, he must have heard her talking to Joe. "Listen, Zachary, I can explain."

"No need. I heard it all."

"You did?"

"Yeah. I followed you. Thought it might be fun to play a little prank. But then I saw how fast you were walking, how you kept looking around, suspiciously. I could tell you knew exactly where you were going, and that made me more curious. It didn't take long for someone as 'unobservant' as I am to figure it out."

Sam felt strangely nervous, something she'd never felt around Zach before. "So," she said, slowly. "What are you going to do?"

He frowned a little and said, "Nothing. What did you think I'd do? Report you or something? I mean, you're right. The old guy isn't hurting anything, and he needs a place to stay. We're essentially protecting a ghost town, here. You made him promise not to bring anybody else." He shrugged.

"Well, thanks. And I'm sure Joe thanks you, too."

"And I thank you."

Sam frowned and said, "What are you thanking me for?"

"For proving me right. That I'm not the only person who isn't like those people on the internet."

Sam smiled sheepishly and Zachary could almost swear that she was blushing a little.

"We better hurry," he said. "Ollie and David will be in soon."

They rode back to the security office in silence, and neither of them were thrilled to see the addition of two vehicles in the office parking lot.

"Shit," Sam muttered as they parked.

The two men were sitting on the steps, smoking. One was a grizzled-looking guy in his sixties. The other, a washed-out thirty-something. Both had only a passing acquaintance with a razor. The bullshit started up the instant they left the truck.

"Whoo-wee!" the younger man said. "Looks like somebody's been having a good time tonight, Ollie." Then, to Sam and Zachary, he said, "Y'all lovebirds out there feathering your nest?"

"Go fuck yourself, David," Sam said. "We were on patrol. You know, that thing you dipshits never do."

"Hey, easy now, Sam," the older man, Ollie, said. He moved aside to allow Zachary past them to the door. Once Zachary unlocked it, David shoved past him to get inside. Zachary sighed and looked at Ollie, who only shrugged. "No, please, after you," Zachary said. Ollie nodded, then, and walked past them. Sam stood waiting.

"After you," Zachary said. She grinned as she went in.

Inside the office, Ollie said, "Anything we need to know?"

Sam glanced at Zachary.

"No. There was a concern that the fence had been breached again, but we checked it out and the patch is still in place."

"What was the concern?" Ollie asked.

"Kyle found a shoe," Zachary said.

David was leaning back in his chair, propping his feet on the card table. "Who gives a fuck about a fuckin' shoe?"

"Well," Sam said, "if the fuckin' shoe belongs to a fuckin' intruder it's sort of the fuckin' thing it's our fuckin' job to check the fuck out, don't you think?"

David glared at her.

"Luckily for us, there's no evidence of any kind of break in. Probably some kids threw it over the fence or something."

"Or the old homeless fuck is back," David said.

Zachary said, "No, we did a very thorough search. There's nobody out there."

Sam swallowed hard.

"Bet you did," David said with a leer.

"Truck keys?" Ollie said. Sam took them from her pocket and handed them to the older man.

"Have a good night," she said.

Ollie nodded. David was already in Rebecca's office, starting up her computer to spend his shift watching YouTube. But Sam was okay with that. For once, she was completely fine with the night crew's inept laziness.

She turned and waved to Zachary on her way out the door.

As she descended the steps to the parking lot, Zachary said, "Hey, Sam, wait up."

She stopped on the steps. "You think everything's going to be okay tonight?" he asked.

"With these two on the job? How could you doubt it?"

He considered that and laughed.

They were halfway to their cars when Sam said, "So ... What do you do when you're not here, Zachary?"

"You mean when I'm NOT surfing the internet for sick crap like you do?"

"Exactly!" she said with a laugh.

"Hate to break it to you, but my life is pretty boring. I'm basically in class or studying whenever I'm not here."

"Bet you're a straight-A student."

"I'm not," he said grimly. "That's why I have to study so hard. But my dad says that's what makes all the difference."

"What does?"

"The hard work. He's got this quote by Thomas Jefferson that he always repeated to me, growing up. 'The harder you work, the luckier you get.'"

Sam grinned and said, "Hey, I kind of like that."

"Yeah, me too. See you tomorrow?"

"Same bat time, same bat place," she said, swinging her arms and lamely clapping her hands together. She felt like she should say something else, something more, but the silence stretched on to the point that any addition would only seem awkward.

"Well," Zachary said. "Good night."

"G'night!"

Zachary looked back at her once to wave as he got into his car, but she was getting into her car then, too.

{blank-top-faded-text}

11

Other neighborhoods around Shadow Vista, real ones, glowed in the night. There was a kind of aura formed not only by streetlight, but by cars and even the occasional light from inside some houses, even when it was this late. Shadow Vista, though, was aptly named. Here it was fuckin' dark. The buildings, without any electricity, seemed to eat up any ambient light.

Though he would never say it aloud, it freaked Tyler's shit right the fuck out. He wasn't a baby or nothing, he was 14, but he didn't like it. And Austin, who was only a year older but acted as if he was, like four billion years older, would call him a homo or whatever if he even hesitated going out at night to Shadow Vista.

Night was when it was safe, though. The little rent-a-pigs at night were a couple of fat pussies, and they had never been out of their little trailer as far as Tyler knew. That's why Austin always wanted to come.

He'd score some weed off Bobbie at school, and sometimes a titty mag, and they'd come out and hang. One time they managed to talk Jess Nielson and her cousin Tiffany to come out, too. Even went through a bunch of crazy shit to get a couple bottles of Boone's Farm, and it looked like shit was gonna get real, but the girls got spooked by the place at night, too.

And girls getting spooked in a theater is one thing. That's the fun kind of spooked. That's when they want to snuggle in a little closer, squish their tits all up on you.

For real spooked isn't fun.

Not for girls, and not for Tyler.

And tonight? Austin didn't seem all that into it, either.

They'd scoped out the scene by the security trailer to make sure the piggies were still there. Then, on their way to the usual spot they crawled through, they saw a section of fence about ten feet wide that had been knocked flat.

"Sweet!" Austin said. When they climbed through their usual place, they had to worry about the sharp edges of chain link getting caught in their clothes. Or scratching their face. But this? Hell, they could ride their bikes right the fuck over the top of it.

Still, both boys hesitated, realizing at the same time that maybe it meant they weren't alone here. And while they were never really alone, what with the rent-a-piggies fucking off in the security trailer, those guys were harmless. They weren't leaving the trailer for nothing. Whoever else was here? Maybe they weren't harmless. And if the boys needed help? The piggies still weren't leaving that trailer for nothing.

"You sure about this?" Tyler asked.

"Fuck yeah. Why? You wanna run home to mommy?"

"No, but what if someone else is here?"

"Fuck 'em," Austin said as he jumped on his bike and rode over the fence into the abandoned subdivision.

With a sigh, Tyler followed.

Inside the nearly finished house at 3512 Trellman Place, Joe Washington woke with a start. That, in itself, was nothing new. He hadn't had what most civilians would consider a good night's sleep for the better part of 50 years. Not since well before he found himself on the streets.

Years ago, after the war and all the protests and all that, he'd mentioned it to the attending doc at the V.A. The little shit had looked over Joe's files, mentioned the injuries he'd sustained in combat, and said, "That was a long time ago. I know sometimes it's hard for guys like you to let it go."

Guys like him? Let it go? People always loved to say things like that. Let it go. They never told you how.

How to wake up in the night with the stink of jungle in your nostrils and your wife's throat in your grip and wondering where the hell you are and why the hell you're still breathing when so many others aren't. They don't tell you what you're supposed to do when the only thing you're qualified to do anymore is crawl in the damned muck and hunt other human beings.

They don't tell you what to do when your wife leaves and your kids don't call.

They don't tell you what to do when the pain meds stop working.

But according to your training, you survive. Even when you don't want to and there's no reason to keep on doing it.

Survive. It's programmed in your DNA.

So, when Joe woke up in the middle of the night, he wasn't sure where he was for a moment, but that was nothing new. What was new was the giggling. The sound of breaking glass.

Then he remembered. He was in Shadow Vista, the kind of neighborhood he could never afford if it hadn't been abandoned. And those sounds? Must be intruders. Vandals, from the sound of it. And he wasn't about to cotton to no vandals.

He grabbed his baseball bat, then slipped on his hoodie, zipped it up and crept into the backyard, quietly.

The sounds were still there. Sporadic. Less than a klick away, easy, and they didn't seem to be coming any closer.

Joe stepped into the shadows of an oak tree in the yard to take a leak. It seemed to him that, these days, he must've pissed at least 20 times a night. Dribbles every damned time. Growing old wasn't for wusses, that was for sure.

Another pop of breaking glass, followed by another high-pitched giggle.

Joe walked to the edge of the patio, crossed the threshold of the gate and peeked around the corner, searching for signs of movement. He could've sworn he saw a bulky figure standing in the shadows down the block, but he rubbed his tired eyes and the shape was gone.

Another crash sounded, followed by a victorious whoop.

"Little bastards," Joe muttered to himself.

He moved down the sidewalk, as quietly as he could, his grip on the bat high and tight.

There, across the street and down nearly half a block, he could see the silhouettes of two boys. Teenagers. He saw them crouch, pick up rocks from the ground near their feet, and stand again to throw them at the windows of the houses. He heard several of the stones bounce dully off of the siding, but one struck lucky and shattered the glass.

"Little fuckin' bastards," Joe said again. He felt a kind of rage deep inside, welling up, filling him with a strength he hadn't felt in years. For Joe Washington, life was about following the rules. He'd been told that if you worked hard and you did what you were supposed to do, well, America was your oyster.

And that, it turned out, was a lie. But it had been a beautiful lie, he thought, and one that had been worth it. He never regretted for a moment the things he'd done for his country. But these little shits. They thought the rules didn't apply to them. They thought it was funny to tear down someone else's hard work. And for Joe, that was about the most intolerable thing he could imagine.

Because it was like they were tearing him down, too.

So he followed the little bastards as they rode their little bikes (bikes their parents had probably given them, no strings attached) through the shadows of the neighborhood. And they were weaving back and forth and acting like a couple of damned idiots. Probably drunk or high or both, knowing kids these days.

And then they stopped very abruptly, and so did Joe.

He'd been good at tracking, way back in 'Nam, and it turned out that was a skill like ... well, like riding a bike. He stayed in the deepest shadows and he kept his mouth shut.

And he kept the bat down by his side, so no light would reflect off the aluminum, not that there was much light to begin with.

Except that there was.

From a lantern across the street. Hooded, but in this darkness, as bright as a full moon. And in the stillness that enveloped him he could hear a repetitive scraping. Like digging. Digging in rock. Or gravel.

He could barely make out the kids, crouched low, hunching behind their bikes as if that could protect them.

Other than that, Joe couldn't see shit, so he moved in closer. He stuck close to the ground, old training taking over effortlessly. And though his knees protested, they did their work, carrying him silently and, for his age, fairly swiftly, until he was hunched alongside a dumpster across from both the boys on one side and the sound of digging on the other.

And from here he could see the digger, dressed in heavy overalls, boots, gloves, and a red ski mask. In spite of how cold it was, this fellow was overdressed.

The digger stopped digging, stood tall to stretch his back for a long moment, and then walked over to a nearby wheelbarrow. There was something there in that wheelbarrow, something that seemed heavy from the way the digger strained.

Then the rays of the lantern fell upon it and Joe heard the sharp intake of breath from one of the boys near him. The other boy, the one who looked a little older, slapped his hand over the younger boy's mouth in an instant. Joe still held his breath because he was certain the digger must have heard them. But nothing in the heavily cloaked figure's movements seemed to suggest that he did. And that was good news for both the boys and Joe, because, in the lantern light, what both the boys and Joe could see clear as day was that the wheelbarrow had a body in it.

- 13 -

The body was a young woman, dressed in office clothes, like she'd been a secretary or something. Joe could see from here that her stockings had massive runs in them and her blouse was torn, exposing a lace bra.

None of that was what had made the kid gasp, though. That would have been her face. Her eyes. What had been her eyes, anyway. Huge crimson X's had been carved there, blinding the woman if she'd been alive. The frenzy with which the job had been done, though, told Joe there was no life left in the girl.

The digger leaned hard against the handles and tipped the barrow to one side. The body, still pliable at least, spilled into a heap on the ground.

And then the strangest thing happened.

The digger took something from a bag at his feet. A small, soft-looking rectangular package. And he set it down in the hole he'd dug, adjusting it carefully before rolling the woman's corpse into the hole. Then the digger spent several minutes positioning the body's head. It was a pillow he'd put in. Had to be. And now he was making sure the dead woman was laying on it properly.

That was some psycho shit.

After getting the body in the right position, the digger began to pour what looked like a ready-mix cement into the hole, starting with the woman's face. Joe chanced a glance at the boys. They were both frozen in disbelief and fear, and Joe couldn't blame them. Though he had never really thought about it, there was a part of him that had assumed that the days of death and anonymous graves were long behind him. That those sorts of things happened in faraway war zones, but not here. Never in America.

Joe saw a sudden light nearby, and heard a scuffle.

"The fuck are you doing, dumbass?"

"Calling 911!"

"He'll see! He'll fuckin' see!"

The small but brilliant light was the screen of a cell phone and the boys struggled as one of them tried to knock it out of the other's hands or at least cover it and dim the light.

The boy with the phone pulled it away and pressed the dial button. From where he was, Joe could even hear the dial tone.

"They'll bust US for trespassing, idiot!" the older boy hissed as he snatched the phone and ended the call.

"Nobody's going to care about that. We might even be heroes for reporting this."

"Just leave me out of it. Leave me the fuck out of it."

The younger boy wrestled his phone away and began walking back toward their bikes.

Joe nearly gave up his position to tell the boys that their argument, hissed whispers and all, was still making entirely too much noise, but with the boys splitting up, there was silence. The quiet, the darkness, rushed in like water in a flash flood.

There was something strange about it all, something wrong.

It only took him a moment to figure out what that something was: the digger was gone.

"Oh, shit," the older boy said, realizing the same thing only moments after Joe had.

The younger boy was now perhaps 30 feet down the sidewalk, and Joe could hear him muttering to himself.

"Tyler," the older boy whispered. "Wait!"

Tyler stopped and spun on his heels to face the older boy. In an exaggerated, and too-loud stage whisper, he said, "WHAT?"

The shadows behind the boy coalesced into the form of a large, imposing figure. Before either Joe or Austin could shout a warning, the digger's shovel swung down in a sharp arc and made a ringing crack as it slammed into the back of Tyler's skull.

The boy made a horrible gurgling rasp, his knees gave out, and he landed on his face. One of the boy's feet spasmed, making staccato taps on the pavement.

Joe figured later that the other kid, Austin, must have spent several seconds staring in horror at his friend's death spasms. That was why he didn't turn and run immediately. That was why he didn't see that the digger was after him, too.

The figure was quick and moved with a loping, almost feline grace that would have been impressive if not for its dark motives. The figure covered the distance between Tyler's fallen form and the other boy in mere seconds. By the time he realized he was in danger, it was almost too late.

But there is power and speed in youth, and the boy

veered out of the killer's grasp, evading a wild swing of the shovel, and sprinted not toward the fence or his bike, but deeper into the darkened neighborhood.

Joe felt like a damned coward, and maybe that's all he was after all, but his heart was beating in his chest in a way that it never had, even in the bad days, even deep in the jungle, and he was having a hard time catching his breath.

He told himself that the boy would be fine, that he was fast, and that Joe himself wouldn't be able to do anything other than to offer himself to the shovel-wielding killer, which may or may not have helped the kid anyway.

He told himself that, but he couldn't help hating himself a little bit, too. He didn't have much of anything that was worth a damn in this life, but he had his service, and that was something he always thought of as a defining characteristic. Service. Helping those who needed help.

And here he was cowering in the dark like a rat, heart pounding and bladder aching. And it wasn't right, dammit.

He took several gulps of air through his mouth, put a hand to his chest as if securing his rogue heart back in place, and set out after the boy.

Austin couldn't chance a look back. He'd seen enough movies to know that was when the bad guy got you. You'd run and run and then you'd look back and he'd be right there. Like there was never anything you could have done to get away. Like it was inevitable that you were dead meat.

And it was lame to admit, sure, but he didn't want to die. Not like he had any great plans yet, other than trying to get in Tiffany Goldacre's pants, but dammit that was as good a goal as anybody's wasn't it? Other people got to keep on going, living goofy lives and getting drunk and high and making out with girls and stuff. Why shouldn't he? He hadn't done anything wrong.

Tyler hadn't done anything wrong, either, though.

And his eyes were burning, and he didn't know where he was going. He wished his brother was there. He was ROTC and he would've known what to do. He wanted his brother, his dad, hell, even his mom. Someone. Anyone.

And without even meaning to, without even thinking about it, he looked back. The guy with the shovel wasn't right behind him, like Jason or Freddy or something, but he was close enough. Close enough that Austin felt a momentary heat as his bladder let go and he pissed himself like a baby.

Then his foot tangled in something and he was down.

He'd winced involuntarily, but his face bounced off something soft. That was luck, wasn't it?

Until he realized that he'd fallen on the dead body.

He was in the hole, the grave, and the woman's dead, mutilated face was only an inch away. He could smell her. Perfume and toothpaste, shampoo and something awful. Death. She couldn't be rotting already, could she? He didn't know, but he knew that this was what death smelled like. That it had gotten into him and he would never forget it.

And he screamed then, breathing in all the smells of her and wanting to be sick from it. But without even meaning to, he pushed himself up to his knees and then to his feet. And though his ankle was really hurting from the fall, he broke into a run. A pretty good run, he thought. But the killer was there, somewhere.

Joe had stuck close to the shadows, hugging the wall of one of the houses, but he stepped into the pale-yellow light and was about to call out to the boy on the ground when he heard something scraping against the concrete. The digger was there, in the yard with the boy. A trick of light and shadow, but a startling one. One moment, the masked killer hadn't been there, but now he most certainly was, chasing after the other boy, who was running away as fast as he could.

Not fast enough.

The digger swung the shovel and the boy's head snapped forward. He threw his arms out reflexively, but he was limp before he hit the ground and slid to a stop.

The masked figure stopped behind him and stood still for a moment, as if to be sure the boy wasn't going to move.

Everything inside Joe told him to edge back into the shadows. To close his eyes and forget about this because there was no way to save those boys. Not now. And certainly no way to save himself, if he made himself known. Carefully, he started backwards, between the houses, into deeper shadows.

One foot kicked an empty soda can and it fell over and started rolling down the driveway toward the street.

Joe watched in horror as the can rattled over the concrete and the digger slowly turned toward the sound.

Joe felt his knees go soft, and he held the wall to stay upright.

The soda can reached the gutter and stopped.

The digger stared toward the shadows for a moment longer, then went to the back of the van and took out a flashlight.

Joe turned and ran away from the horror. Some part of him heard, or imagined hearing, the heavy footsteps of the digger, already after him, already gaining.

He didn't look back to see if it was a paranoid fantasy or the horrible truth. He ran. Even though his knees were pudding and his lungs were white fire.

Joe's brain scrambled to come up with a plan. He wasn't stronger or faster or more ruthless than some masked child killer, but he had experience and knowledge and a kind of animal survival instinct.

He'd been sneaking around this project long enough to evade detection most times. He knew this place. Did he know it better than the killer? He thought so, but was he really willing to bet his life on that? What choice did he have?

He emerged from between two houses onto Witney Circle. This was where the boys had been because nearly all the windows were broken out. They had done the most damage to 1224.

Joe ran toward it and climbed through the front window into the living room. His hand pressed into a jagged piece of glass still in the frame and he bit his tongue to stop himself from crying out as he flopped to the floor.

Once he caught his breath, he carefully peeked over the sill.

For a long time, the night was still. The shadows in the other houses were dark and motionless.

And then he was there—the digger—separating from the shadows and strolling to the middle of the cul-de-sac. He raised one arm and extended his index finger, pointing at the houses and turning slowly, like a weathervane.

Joe held his breath and watched, waiting for the finger to find him in the darkness. Before it did, he ducked again and pressed himself flat along the wall below the window. He started thinking about those boys again and told himself not to. He had to stay in the present, keep himself as sharp as possible, because as far as he was concerned, he wasn't out of the woods yet.

Later, he could blame himself. Later, he could replay the night 10,000 different ways and realize how he might have saved those poor innocents if only he had done something more.

But not now. Thinking of that stuff now could still get him killed. And what good would it all be, then?

Still holding his breath, Joe lifted his head until his eyes cleared the sill.

The digger was gone. Or so Joe hoped.

Then he heard an engine roar to life in the distance. He heard doors slam and saw shadows flicker as headlights shone between the houses on the far side of the circle.

Quickly, Joe stood up and lifted himself back over the sill. He was careful to avoid the broken glass this time. He needed to do something about that cut in his hand. But first, he had to check on those boys.

Eyes wide, he stuck to the shadows (just in case) as he crossed the circle and went back between the houses onto the other street.

The van was gone. So were the boys. And, Joe noticed now with a shiver, so were their bikes.

The white van drove back to the spot in the fence where the boys had come through. The digger steered slowly over the piece on the ground, then onto the street and away from the subdivision.

Flat acres of unused farmland separated Shadow Vista from the other neighborhoods nearby. The roads between them and the nearby freeway had been built with future development in mind. Several spots along the way were marked with large wooden signs promising more homes in the future.

Until then, however, this area was almost completely dark. The digger assumed the boys had not come very far. Their BMX bikes weren't built for distance. They also didn't have lights or reflectors. Neither boy had been wearing a helmet, either, even though they should have been. All of this fit perfectly with what the digger planned to do.

Halfway down the rural road, in between streetlights, the digger stopped the van and got out.

They opened the double doors at the back and pulled the boys and their bikes down to the pavement. Then they closed the doors, got back inside the van and drove away, taillights receding into the dark like sparks from a campfire.

Then the lights brightened as the van braked. The reverse lights came on as the van backed into a three-point turnaround.

A moment later, the headlights stabbed through the dark and the van sat, idling.

Austin groaned as the cold pavement finally brought him back to consciousness. He blinked and reached back to touch the knot on his head. At the same moment he remembered being hit with the shovel, he realized that he wasn't where he had been knocked out. "What the hell, man?"

He lifted his head slightly and saw Tyler nearby, both their bikes in a tangle between them. They were outside the subdivision somehow. Had they ridden here?

"Tyler," he said as he sat up.

Behind him, he heard an engine rev and he turned slowly, squinting against the headlights.

His first thought was that whoever was in that car had stopped to help them. But why had they stopped so far back?

He used one hand to shield his eyes from the light and felt ice water running down his back. It wasn't a car. It was a van. The white van. The one driven by that maniac who had attacked them.

The tires suddenly screeched as they spun and the van rocketed toward him.

Austin jumped to his feet. He grabbed one of the bikes and yanked it free of the other, then hopped on and started pedaling.

The light at his back got twice as bright. The bastard had put his high beams on.

Austin dared to look over his shoulder as the van drove over the other bike and then over Tyler. The bike spun away, but Tyler's body somehow caught on the running board and was dragged for ten feet before tearing free and going under the rear tires with an awful thumping.

The sound of his body being crushed was the worst thing Austin had ever heard. Even worse than his baby sister's crying after he had accidentally hit her in the face with a softball.

Austin pedaled harder. He knew he was dead for sure if he stayed in the road, so he steered to the right. The van would have a hard time keeping up with him in the field out there. His bike, on the other hand, was made for it. Then, at the last moment, he remembered the drainage ditch over that edge and cranked the handlebars left as hard as he could.

He raced toward the opposite side and tried to jump the curb onto the sidewalk. But his back wheel caught the edge and he had to put both feet down to keep his balance.

Before he could pull his bike up, the left front bumper of the van clipped his back tire and spun him around. His head caught the driver's side mirror and the glass shattered.

Austin hit the sidewalk and slid.

At the same time, the van's tires screeched again as it skidded to a halt.

Unbelievably, Austin got to his feet. In a daze, he stumbled back the way he had come, toward Tyler.

The van's engine revved again as the reverse lights came on and it backed toward him at high speed.

Confused, Austin turned around, just in time to meet

the rear of the van with his face, slamming him backward to the pavement with a sickening crack.

The van idled for a moment before shifting into drive and pulling away slowly. A beat later, the dark returned and the crickets started singing again.

- 15 -

Zachary pulled into his usual parking spot, fingers drumming on the steering wheel to a '60s rock song. The lot seemed emptier than usual for this time of day. Sam's Bug wasn't here, but that was no surprise. He looked at his hair in the rearview mirror, checked his teeth, practiced his most winning smile.

And, after jogging from the car to the entrance singing to himself, he waved cheerily to Bob on his way to the time clock. Bob was on the phone and only wagged an irritated finger at Zachary, but that didn't bother him at all. He ducked into Rebecca's office to say hello to her as well, but saw that it was empty. His caffeine-deprived brain realized, too late, that her Civic had been missing from the lot.

He looked back to Bob, still on the phone, and heard him saying, "Are you sure? If you need a day, I totally understand. It'd be hard, but we'll get by somehow." He grinned, baring teeth stained by decades of nicotine. "Listen, you take care of yourself today. That's a direct order, y'hear?" He grinned again and said, "All right, now. We'll see you tomorrow."

Zachary leaned into Bob's office and said, "Was that Rebecca? Is she sick?"

Bob's grin faded so fast that Zachary wondered if it had ever really been there or if he had imagined it.

"Yes. And no, she isn't sick."

"Well, what's going on? Is she okay?"

"About as okay as a young lady can be after seeing what she saw on her way in today."

Zachary frowned and took a step closer, lowering himself into one of the cheap folding chairs set before Bob's desk.

"There was a terrible hit and run accident last night," Bob said, taking a cigarette from his shirt pocket and lighting it. Zachary had never seen him smoke inside. He always went out, even in the coldest weather. "Rebecca came in early to catch up on paperwork and found two kids dead in the road about a mile from here."

"What happened?"

"Cops said it looked like the kids were riding without lights or helmets. Somebody in some kind of larger vehicle, a truck or van they said, plowed right into them."

"That's terrible."

Bob nodded.

Zachary leaned back in his chair and took a deep breath. He couldn't believe this. "Fuck," he said.

"Watch your language," Bob said.

"Shit," Zachary said sheepishly. "Sorry."

Bob scowled even more. Zachary kept his mouth shut.

"Anyway," Bob said, "it was apparently pretty gruesome. And for a gal like Rebecca, well, it shook her up some."

"Totally," Zachary said.

"Did you guys happen to see that homeless guy around?"

Zachary swallowed hard. "Uh ... No. Never did. Why?"

Bob stared at him for a long time, and Zachary felt uncomfortable. "Are you sure you guys didn't see anything?"

"Yeah, I'm sure. I'm only thinking about Rebecca is all."

Bob sighed. "Right. About that. A couple of things you need to know. First is: no girl likes desperate. And you positively reek of desperation."

"Hey..."

"And the other is that you can't go running after something that's not yours to begin with."

Zachary frowned. "What's that supposed to mean?"

Bob's office door opened and Kyle walked in.

"Hear anything back from the cops, Pop?" Kyle said with his mouth full. That and the fact that he'd called Bob "Pop" in front of another employee had Bob scowling again. Zachary was glad that it wasn't only him.

Then he noticed what was in Kyle's hand. It was a pack of Oreo cookies. The very same cookies that were causing Kyle to talk with his mouth full.

And while it was possible that this pack was totally innocent, Zachary couldn't help but remember the pack that he and Sam had seen in the house on Katz Parkway, the one that had also contained the very creepy (and sticky) doll that had fallen on him.

"What's your problem?" Kyle was saying, and Zachary realized that both Kyle and Bob were staring at him intently.

"Nothing. Just thinking again about the accident."

"Yeah, man. Some crazy shit right there. And I don't think it's an accident. No sirree, I don't."

"I'm guessing you didn't find him either," Bob said.

"Who?" Kyle said, expelling a tiny cloud of chocolate crumbs, a few of which landed on Zachary's shoulder.

He grimaced.

"The homeless guy!" Bob said.

"Oh. Right. No, I didn't."

"Did you even look for him?"

"Yes, Dad. I did."

Bob took a deep breath and stood. "All right. Let's go."

- **16** -

Zachary followed the two men out of Bob's office. Bob turned and said, "You and Sam keep looking, okay? And be careful. Be on high alert for anything out of the ordinary."

Zachary nodded.

"And be sure to tell Ollie and David the same thing."

Zachary nodded again.

After Bob and Kyle left, Zachary went to the break room. He damn sure wasn't patrolling by himself, so he sat down to wait for Sam, took out his phone and opened Facebook to do the same search he'd done dozens of times before.

Rebecca Summers. The profile pic was the generic black silhouette they give you if you haven't uploaded a photo, but he knew this was his coworker.

"To see what she shares with friends, send her a friend request," the profile read. And, like always, he hovered over the friend request button for a good two minutes before cursing to himself and closing the app.

He glanced at the clock, brought up Facebook again, and searched for Samantha Wong.

Lots of profiles had that name, but he found Sam's by her picture. It looked like a shot from a birthday party. She had her arm around a blond girl and they both had daiquiri glasses in their hands. They were laughing.

Zachary grinned. He clicked on her photos. There was an album of bowling pictures, a few shots of her visiting her grand-mother at a retirement home, a series of Sam teaching her niece how to ride a bike, some shots from a visit to the beach.

The front door opened.

"Shit!" Zachary said, shoving his phone into his pocket.

Sam looked around and said, "The one time I'm actually early, and the boss isn't here to see it?"

"Yeah, they, uh, left as soon as I got here. And Rebecca didn't come in at all today."

Sam hung her bag on a wall hook and said, "Because of the hit and run?"

"You know about that?"

"Yeah, it's all over the news. They said a female employee of a nearby business found the bodies. Since there's not much out here, I figured it must be her."

"It was on the news?"

"Of course! What did Bob say about everything?"

"Just that she's shaken up and she'll be back tomorrow."

Sam leaned against the table and said, "Really? Man, I'm surprised she's not milking it for at least one more day."

Zachary looked down at the ratty carpet.

"Oh, I'm sorry," Sam said. "I forgot. You don't like me cutting on your little crush?"

He shrugged. "Whatever, Sam."

"Y'know ... you build up this little fantasy in your head, but not everybody is who you think they are."

"I can see that," he said, facing her.

Sam put a hand to her chest as if wounded. "Well, touché."

He smiled faintly.

"And you're right. I'm making some assumptions of my own. Forgive me?"

He nodded.

"Good. Now help me get the groceries out of my car."

"Groceries?"

"For Joe."

Sam trotted down the steps to the parking lot, and Zachary followed her. Once at her VW, Zachary had a sinking realization.

"Shit."

She looked at him, read the expression on his face, and said, "Let me guess. Jughead took off with the keys because you forgot to get them from him again."

"The whole hit and run thing really kind of threw me."

"Welp. I guess we're taking my car tonight."

"You know the rules, Sam. We're only supposed to have the company car on subdivision property."

"Hey, dude. Not my fault. Besides, it's supposed to rain tonight. What are you gonna do, let me get all wet and cold?" She batted her eyelashes.

Zachary frowned, but he knew himself well enough to know that he was giving in. "Fine," he said. "I'll go open the gate."

- 17 -

Sam drove through the open gate, stopped, and let Zachary into the passenger seat. "Whoa," he said. Every surface, from the steering wheel and dash, to the seats and floor mats, was painted with psychedelic flowers. Sam's Bug was like a rolling acid trip.

"You like?" she asked, clearly pleased.

"It's ... really something."

"Thanks. It took a lot of work."

"Did you do all this yourself?"

"Me and my sister, yeah. Want us to do your car?"

Zachary laughed. "That's not my car. Not yet, anyway."

Sam glanced at him and said, "What's that mean?"

"It's my dad's. It'll be mine when I graduate."

She glanced at him again, eyebrow raised quizzically.

"Yeah, I know. It's kind of a crappy college graduation gift."

"I never said that."

"Your eyes did."

"Look at you! Finally starting to pay attention."

Zachary shifted in his seat. "Well, hey, you're a good teacher."

"Sorry. That was a shitty thing to say. And sorry for earlier."

He shrugged. "It's okay."

Sam's Bug backfired as they pulled into the driveway of the house on Trellman Place. They got out, retrieving the groceries from the back, and headed through the gate to the backyard.

"Joe!" Sam called. But there was no response.

"Sliding door's open," Zachary said.

They walked to the open patio doors and entered the house.

"Maybe he's sleeping," Zachary said.

She shook her head. "Even if he was, he'd be awake now. Light sleeper. Always on the run."

They put the groceries on the counter and moved through the kitchen to the living room.

"His stuff's still here. You don't think Kyle found him and called the cops, do you?"

Zachary said, "I know he didn't. At least that's what he told Bob. Seemed like he'd forgotten he was supposed to be looking."

Sam glanced around, clearly troubled, and said, "Let's leave the stuff here and drive around. See if we can find him."

"You bet," Zachary said. "That's what Bob told us to do tonight anyway." He puffed himself up, gave her his best stern Bob face, and said, "Find that homeless feller."

Sam snorted. She was still laughing as they left the house.

And nearly walked right into an aluminum baseball bat.

"Joe!" Sam said, dodging backward.

The old man was in bad shape. He was dirtier than usual, and his face seemed sunken somehow, his eyes haunted.

"Oh, sweetie," he groaned. "Thank Jesus it's you."

Sam put an arm around the old man. Zachary was amazed by her compassion and repulsed at the same time. The old man's smell would have kept Zachary from showing Joe the same human kindness Sam was showing him now.

"What's wrong, Joe?" she said.

Tears welled in his eyes. "Oh, it was terrible."

"What was?"

"Those ... Those boys. I-I tried to stop it. I tried. But I was too slow. Too slow and too ... too damn scared."

"Boys?"

Joe looked around, suddenly panicking. "We need to get inside. Maybe you can help me pack up my things. I need to find another place. Keep moving. In case he comes back."

"In case who comes back?"

"The killer!" Joe hissed. "Terrible what he did to those boys."

Zachary could hardly believe it. "You saw the accident?"

Joe barked a dismissive laugh. "Accident? Wasn't no accident. I saw him hit them."

"What kind of car was it?" Sam asked.

"Not a car," the old man said. "A shovel."

Zachary and Sam traded confused glances, then followed the old man inside.

Sam asked Joe to start from the start, so he did, spitting out what seemed to Zachary like little more than the confused ramblings of a drunk old man. But Sam kept at it, picking up little pieces and putting them together, saying his own words back to him until a picture began to form.

Despite its clarity, Zachary was still skeptical. Joe saw it on his face. "You don't believe me, I can tell."

"I do," Sam said.

"He doesn't!" Joe said, pointing at Zachary with his bat.

Zachary started to say something, but Sam glared at him.

"He does," she said. "We both do. We have to."

"No, we don't," Zachary said.

"Yes, we do. He's an eyewitness to a crime. We can't say it's not true until we can prove it's not true."

Joe held up his injured hand. He'd wrapped it with paper towels, but the blood had soaked through. "Proof!" he said.

"Exactly," Sam said. "And once we can confirm your version, then we'll need to tell the police."

Joe stiffened. "No," he said. "They'll lock me up again!"

"They won't," Sam said, putting her hand on his shoulder. "I won't let them."

The old man smiled weakly.

"Let us take a look around," Sam said. "See what we can find out. You stay here until we get back."

"Okay," Joe said. "But be careful."

18

Halfway down the front walk, Zachary said, "Do you really believe him?"

Sam frowned. "Why would he lie?"

"I'm not saying he's lying. But I know you like the old guy, and maybe that's the problem. He's been through a lot of shit in his life. You don't think he could get mixed up?"

She looked at him, her eyes serious. "Not about this."

"Okay," he said, then looked around. "Joe says the house he hid in was in a cul-de-sac. I think Witney Circle is closest."

Sam nodded as they got into her Bug and drove the few blocks before parking again and getting out.

Zachary shook his head when he saw the damage the boys had done. "Punks broke every one of them."

"Joe says the window was completely broken." Sam pointed at the house marked 1224. "What do you think?"

Zachary saw that she was right: the front window of 1224 was more broken than the others. He nodded and they walked closer.

When they were within ten feet of it, he saw the dried

blood caked on the remaining shards of the windowpane. Though he'd been skeptical of Joe's account (mainly because of how confused he'd seemed) Zachary had to admit, so far, anyway, everything the old man had said was panning out.

"Shit," Sam said.

Zachary figured she must've been thinking more or less the same thing.

"Now which way?" Sam said, facing the circle.

In the daylight, the subdivision was a very different place from the subdivision in the pitch black of night. Zachary had learned that lesson more than once. He knew intimately how freaky this place could be. He almost couldn't imagine how much freakier it would be if you knew there was a real killer after you. The thought of it made his stomach roil.

"He said he followed the boys between the houses."

Sam smirked. "That's helpful."

"Maybe we can find the soda can," Zachary said. "The one Joe said he kicked over."

"Good idea." A long rolling peal of thunder sounded overhead. Both of them looked up to see dark clouds approaching. "We better hurry," Sam said.

"Think we should split up?" Zachary said.

Sam looked at him for what felt like a long time. Zachary could tell that she must've been having the same sort of uneasy thoughts he was.

"I guess. But let's stay close, okay?"

"Absolutely."

They searched along the street, leapfrogging each other to check alternating houses. On the street behind Sam's fourth house, she found the soda can in the gutter.

"Found it!" she shouted.

Zachary joined her a moment later. Together they stared at the can. Then they faced the street, searching for signs of where the van might have been.

"C'mon," Zachary said, jogging down the sidewalk until he found a pair of faint tire tracks. When he turned around, Sam was crouched by a dark stain on the pavement. Zachary approached her slowly. "Is that...?"

"Looks like it to me," she said.

"Shit."

"Joe saw exactly what he told us," she said as she stood. "Those kids caught that creep burying a body in here. And he killed them to shut them up. Then he took their bodies out and made it look like a hit and run."

Zachary paused. "But how did the van get in? The front gate is the only way, and we're the only ones with keys."

"Not the only ones," Sam said.

Zachary snorted. "You think Ollie or David did it? They never leave the office."

"No. There's a way more obvious answer."

"Bob?"

Sam groaned.

Zachary stared at her, not understanding. And then he did. "You think it's Kyle?"

"It fits, don't you think? I mean, he's fucking a cold, clammy doll in an abandoned subdivision when nobody's looking. What if that doll isn't enough for him anymore?"

Zachary paced as he thought it over. He had to admit that it did make a certain sense, except...

"Look ... there's no conceivable universe where I'm president of the Kyle fan club or anything, but ... I mean ... yes, he thinks he's a tough guy and yes, he's into blow up dolls or whatever ... but a killer? Someone who kills teenage boys?"

Sam put her hands on his shoulders. The contact was both strange and oddly welcome. "Those kids wouldn't have been his preferred target. Remember: they caught him in the act and HAD to die. That made all that shit a matter of necessity, not choice. Think about it. What if this wasn't the first time? How many other bodies could be out here?"

Zachary looked around, slowly. There was an awful lot of land. And most of it? Nobody would notice if it was disturbed. The place looked all dug up anyway.

Shit.

"It's perfect, isn't it?"

Zachary didn't say anything. He was too busy being simultaneously amazed and nauseated.

Kyle?

Douchebag Kyle?

Then Sam said, "I remember about a year ago, there was this guy who killed his wife. Buried her in his backyard, then put a brand-new patio right on top. It was all over the news."

"Because they caught him," Zachary said.

"I know. He was shifty as fuck, and neighbors saw the concrete mixer in front of the house. That guy wasn't exactly a criminal genius. But out here...?"

Zachary said, "Okay, but what about those boys? Why didn't he hide their bodies?"

Sam thought for a minute and said, "Because if they went missing there'd be a search of the area. Including this area. But making it look like a hit and run out there keeps the cops from coming in here."

Zachary nodded. "Okay. Let's see what we can find."

The thunder roared again, but the two of them ignored it, pushing forward to check the various houses and yards for any sign of disturbance. Before they got very far, though, the rain began to fall, erasing any potential clues.

Hiding under an overhang, Sam looked at the rain-filled street and said, "Guess we should get back to the office, huh?"

They ran to her Bug. Once safely inside, Sam put on the heater and shivered until it began to spit out warm air.

"What now?" Zachary asked.

"Obviously, we need to find some proof of something. If we go to the cops with nothing but the account of a confused homeless guy, we'll be the laughingstock of the city. As I'm sure you're aware, they don't exactly have a high opinion of us private security types, anyway."

"True. But please tell me you're not planning on digging up a bunch of patios."

Sam shook her head absentmindedly. Then she said, "I was thinking about some stuff I saw on the news last month or so."

"Are you really serious about all this?" There wasn't any reason to doubt her, but the whole situation seemed so bizarre. Up to this point, his most stressful moment on the job was the time a squirrel got stuck in a storm door.

"Aren't you?" she asked. "What happened to all that shit about helping people and catching bad guys?"

"I'm not a cop," Zachary said. "Maybe I never will be."

Sam grinned. "Don't worry. I'll be your back up."

"You will?"

She nodded and leaned in toward him.

Wait, what was this?

Zachary tentatively leaned toward her, too.

He never really thought he had much of a chance with Sam, but hey, if there was magic in the air or whatever, he was down. She wasn't closing her eyes. Was that a thing?

Had he misread the entire situation? Fuck, was he being a giant idiot?

He didn't care. She looked pretty cute all drenched and shivering, and given all the crazy shit of the day, maybe what they both needed was to be close. As close to her as he was now.

Then something struck the window. Hard.

19

They both jumped, then saw it was only Joe, standing out there like a drowned rat.

Sam rolled her window down and said, "You scared the shit out of me, Joe! What is it?"

The old man's eyes were wide but clear. "I remember where I saw the van!"

Sam said, "Okay, where?"

"It was here! Right here!"

Sam glanced over at Zachary and said, "We kinda figured that much out. Jump in. We'll give you a ride back to the house."

Joe slid into the rear seat and looked around while he squeezed rainwater out of his hair and beard.

"Ain't this something?" he said, staring at the artwork inside Sam's Bug. "Reminds me of the Summer of Love. In more ways than one."

"Oh yeah?"

"Yes ma'am. Best days of my life. San Francisco, back in '67. You kids know what I'm talking about?"

Sam smiled. "As a matter of fact, I do." Then she flipped

on the stereo and fiddled with her phone until Jefferson Airplane's "Somebody to Love" erupted from the speakers.

Sam glanced over in time to see Zachary staring wide-eyed at her stereo.

"What's the matter?" she asked. "Not your thing?"

He looked at her and grinned. "No. This is totally my thing. I'm surprised it's your thing!"

"Not as surprised as I am that it's your thing!" she said.

She glanced in the rearview mirror and saw Joe leaning back in his seat with a huge grin on his face.

After they pulled into the driveway of the house on Trellman Place, Joe slowly climbed out and, still smiling, waved to them as he walked through the gate into the backyard.

Back in the office, they dried off and then Sam used Rebecca's computer to search through several news sites before finding what she'd been looking for. She angled the monitor toward Zachary and said, "This is what I was talking about."

Zachary leaned over her shoulder and looked at the headline and the accompanying photo. "Local College Junior Still Missing." The girl in the photo was blonde, fit, and pretty.

Without thinking, Zachary said, "She looks a bit like Rebecca, don't you think?"

Sam stared at the picture and tapped her lip with a pen. "A bit," she said. "And now that you mention it, so does that sex doll."

Zachary felt a leaden weight sinking in his gut. "Click on that link. The 'Related Articles' one."

Sam did. A list of other stories popped up. Zachary saw one that read, "Police suspect foul play in missing couple case."

"Click on that one."

The page loaded, displaying the story and its photo.

"Holy shit! Look at them. At her."

Sam leaned forward.

"Damn. Looks like our killer definitely has a type."

Zachary nodded. The woman in the photo, though a little older, was also blonde, fit, and pretty. And she bore more than a passing resemblance to their co-worker and Zachary's crush.

"When was this?"

"Last week."

"Shit."

Sam took a deep breath and looked at Zachary. "We have to do something."

"Agreed," Zachary said. "But what?"

"We could start by searching Kyle's Jeep."

"What? How?"

She thought for a minute, then said, "He has to bring the truck keys over anyway, right? I can hide outside. When he brings them in to you, I'll dig around while you keep him busy."

"What are you expecting to find?"

She shrugged. "Dunno. But it's the only thing I can think of right now, so we should try it. Call him."

Zachary groaned. Part of him wanted to follow Sam on her hunch hunt, but another part of him was worried because there was actual danger involved. When Sam raised her eyebrows at him, he took the Rolodex from Rebecca's desk and found Kyle's number. As he dialed, Sam said, "Be casual."

"Oh, I'm casual," Zachary said.

"I mean super casual."

"I will."

"Do you want me to do it?"

Zachary picked up the phone, took a deep breath, and dialed. A few seconds later, he said, "Yo, Kyle?"

Sam furrowed her brow and mouthed the word, "Yo?"

Zachary shrugged and said, "You forgot to leave us the truck keys again, man. Think you could swing 'em by?"

Sam stared at him, but Zachary turned away. "Oh, how'd we do the four o'clock rounds? We walked it. It wasn't bad. But it's raining now."

There was a long silence.

Then Zachary said, "Thanks, Kyle." He hung up and turned to Sam. "He'll be by in a bit."

20

Kyle sighed as he rose from the side of the bed where he'd been sitting and turned off the softcore smut movie playing on his television. The walls of his room were covered in posters of scantily clad ladies, and his eyes slid over them as he picked up his jacket and keys from a chair in the corner. For a moment, he was upset by the interruption. But now he was thinking otherwise. A visit to his girlfriend was always better than what he was getting ready to do.

Passing through the living room on his way to the front door, he saw that his father was still awake, camped out in his easy chair, a beer in one hand, the television remote in the other, and what looked like an episode of "Monster Hunters" on the TV.

"You forgot to leave the truck keys again, didn't you?" Bob asked without looking at him.

"No," Kyle said quickly. "The Jeep needs gas."

"It's raining out. Do it in the morning."

"I'll forget in the morning." And with that, he slipped out the door before his father could say anything else.

It was a short drive to the development. As he got close,

Kyle turned off his headlights and coasted in slow until he could see the lights of the security office.

Sam's VW Bug and Zachary's Camry were in the lot, and Kyle looked at the office windows, trying to see inside. He'd been wondering for a while if Sam and Zachary were fucking, and he had to admit he wouldn't mind catching a glimpse of that action if they were. Sam was no Rebecca, but few were. And hey, T&A was T&A.

But not tonight.

From what he could see, Zachary was staring at Rebecca's computer. And although he didn't see Sam, he knew she had to be in there if Zachary was.

"Good," Kyle whispered, then turned and drove back the way he came, past the front gate.

He drove along the fence toward the northwest corner to the spot where the homeless guy had cut through the fence before. When he'd patched the fence, he'd come up with the idea of making his own gate. That way, he could swing by at times like these and not worry about being spotted by the others.

He'd put wing nuts on the sides of a section of fence between two poles. Unscrewing them allowed him to drop the whole piece flat. With a smile, he got back in the Jeep and drove over it, heading straight to the driveway of 7237 Katz Parkway.

He got the keys from the lock box and opened the front door.

"Honey, I'm home!" he shouted as he went in, cracking up at his own joke, as he always did.

He turned on his flashlight and went upstairs, entering the bedroom at the end of the hall. He quickly slipped the bungee cords off the bedroll in the corner and spread it flat.

"You ready to go, baby?" Kyle laughed again. "What am I talking about? You're always ready to go!"

He opened the closet and carefully brought down the sleeping bag with his doll in it. He placed her carefully on the bedroll and got her positioned exactly the way he liked, taking time to cradle her head tenderly until he got the pillow settled beneath her head.

"There you go," he said, unbuckling his belt and sliding his pants to the floor. "Close your eyes, baby." He reached out and pushed the lids down over the doll's dead, staring eyes.

Slipping the belt free of the loops in his pants, Kyle playfully used the metal prong in the buckle to poke the toy's latex nipples. "You like that, don't you?" he said, grinning, then remembered he didn't have a lot of time. Sam and Zach were waiting for him to bring the keys.

Quickly, he put the belt around his neck and slid the end through the buckle. He pulled it tight, but not too tight. Then he put the end of the belt in the doll's hand and closed his own hand over it, making it look (and feel) like she was the one tugging on it. "Careful now," he said. "You don't wanna hurt me."

As Kyle began thrusting himself into the doll, the shadows behind him suddenly took shape.

It was the digger, dressed as before in black leather gloves, black boots, gray overalls, and a ski mask that looked dyed in dried blood. They stepped forward carefully, head cocked quizzically, watching.

And then they leapt, dropping both knees into the small of Kyle's back hard enough to rupture a kidney, driving the air from his lungs in a surprised, gagging cough.

Kyle's arms thrust out, lifting his upper body as he tried to breathe in again, but before he could, the digger snatched the end of Kyle's belt from the doll's grip and pulled it taut. And though he clawed at it, he could only do so with one hand, the other struggling to hold him upright and take whatever pressure possible off his airway.

The digger leaned back, pulling the belt like an unruly dog's leash, putting considerable weight into the act.

The belt cut deeply into Kyle's skin, crushing his Adam's apple, and compressing his airway enough that he couldn't even wheeze a protest. The skin of his face darkened to deep purple, and he could feel his eyes bulging from their sockets.

Everything went gray in his world, and a taste like ash filled his dry, gaping mouth. Then there was a psychedelic burst of color like fireworks as the blood vessels in his eyes popped, painting the gray world in swirls of crimson that danced before brilliant pinwheels of light overtook it all and his panic, with his heart, ceased.

The masked figure waited until the final twitches of Kyle's dying nerves stopped, then dismounted. They placed the loose end of the belt back in the doll's hand with Kyle's on top, exactly as it had been only moments before.

The figure stood, locked the bedroom door from the inside, and closed it upon exiting.

"What the fuck is taking that douche so long?" Sam said, strolling into Rebecca's office.

Zachary picked up the phone and called Kyle again. When the voicemail answered, he hung up. Then he called the landline.

He knew he'd woken Bob and winced as he said, "Hi Mr. Brashear. It's Zachary Frenkel calling."

"What's wrong?" Bob said on the other end.

"Kyle forgot to leave us the keys again. I called earlier and he said he'd bring them by. But it's been over an hour."

"And he's still not there?"

"No, sir. That's why I'm calling."

"Hang on," Bob said as he took his cellphone out of his shirt pocket and turned it on. After thumbing an app called "Lokator," he tapped an icon labeled "Kyle."

A moment later, a tiny spinning wheel appeared onscreen, then a map. A blinking blue dot appeared on the map, and Bob let out a long sigh.

"I'll be right there," he said and hung up before Zachary could say goodbye.

"What?"

"I don't know," Zachary said. "He sounded weird."

"But he's coming over."

"Yeah."

Zachary stared at Sam.

"What now?"

"Can I ask you something?"

Sam smiled. "You can ask me anything. Whether or not I answer you is another story."

"How do you know so much about all this dark shit? You're like a Wikipedia of weirdness."

Sam laughed. "Wikipedia of weirdness? Did you come up with that?"

Zachary nodded.

"Right now?"

He nodded again.

"All on your own?"

Zachary laughed. "Yeah."

"I like it. Think I'll put it on my business cards. Know why?"

"Why?"

"It spells WOW. As an acronym."

Zach thought about it and shrugged nonchalantly. "I know."

"Dude. You did not."

"Okay, you're right, I didn't. But it's still pretty cool."

"Aaaanyway. I'm the W.O.W. because my dad was a cop, so I learned some dark shit, as you say, from a young age."

"You said was?"

"He died when I was six. This guy he put away got out because of a technical glitch. He found where we lived and he waited outside and he shot my dad. And then he got away."

Zachary stared at her, not knowing what to say.

"For months after, my mom watched the news continuously, hoping to hear they'd caught the guy. She even had my dad's police scanner on at night, when she was sleeping."

"Did they?"

"No. And, watching the news all those years? I sort of got used to it, y'know? The idea that people can do horrible shit and skate. No justice, no accountability."

Zachary sat on the desk beside her and said, "I'm sorry."

She shrugged and went back to looking at the computer screen, but her eyes, despite their hardness, shone with tears.

Anxious to fill the awkward silence, Zachary said, "I know it seems dark sometimes, but I think a lot of that is the news, trying to get ratings. The good stuff doesn't hook people like the bad. But there's plenty of good in the world."

Sam wiped her tears away before they reached her cheeks. "I used to think you were pretty naive," she said.

"Yeah?"

"Yeah. But I know now that you see things in a different way. I always assume people are bad until they proved they aren't. You're the opposite."

"I am?"

"Yes, boy scout. You assume everyone is good and wait until they prove you wrong."

Zachary smiled faintly at that. Sam smiled back at him. Then he cocked his head and looked at the ceiling. "You hear that?"

"I don't hear anything," she said.

"Exactly. Rain's stopped."

"Oh," Sam said, her voice small.

Zachary's eyes met hers again, and he realized for the first time how close they were to each other. Even closer than they had been in the Bug before Joe had interrupted.

He swallowed hard, overcome once more with the strange sudden urge to kiss Sam, and didn't know if that was something she wanted, too, or if it was some goofy crap that '80s movies and bad sitcoms had planted in his brain.

He didn't have time to consider it, though, because an engine revved somewhere outside. Zachary jumped up from his seat and looked through the blinds to see the Tin Star Security truck pull out of its parking spot, driving past Bob's white Ford F-150, lights blinding in the dark lot.

Sam joined him at the window. "Is that Kyle?"

"All I see is Bob's truck. C'mon."

Together they jogged outside in time to see Bob opening the gate. Then, hopping back in the Tin Star truck, he drove into Shadow Vista.

"Should we drive over?" Sam said.

Zachary looked at her for a moment before registering what she'd said. "In your car? No. As weird as Bob gets about that, he'd fire us for sure."

"Then we're walking?"

"Yeah, I mean, it's only a few blocks, right?"

22

Bob pulled up behind Kyle's jeep and threw the truck into park. He got out, bringing his flashlight, and went up the walk and through the front door. He turned on his flashlight, which bathed the vacant house in an eerie, bluish light, and headed to the stairs.

On the second floor, he searched the open rooms, calling out to his son. In answer, there was only the unnatural stillness.

When at last he came to the locked bedroom door, he tried it several times before he said, "Kyle? C'mon, now. I know you're in there. Open up so we can talk about this."

When there was no response, he put his ear to the door and listened. He thought he heard something, but these houses had a way of creaking and complaining all on their own.

Bob felt a hot ball of leaden uneasiness forming in his gut. He'd done tours in active war zones and over ten years as a beat cop. He knew when he was in the presence of death. He hoped he was wrong.

"C'mon, son," he said as he tried the door again. "Open up and let me in. I won't be mad. I promise." He listened for only a moment more before adding, "All right. You've left me no choice. I'm coming in."

He reared back a booted foot and kicked a spot below the doorknob, splintering the jamb and sending the door flying in.

The flashlight trained on the bed almost immediately.

"Oh," he said. Not a word, more like an involuntary sound. "Oh. Oh no."

He moved toward his son and used the blanket to cover his nakedness. There was no need to check for a pulse, and no need to administer aid. The purple color of his face, unseeing eyes, and thick, black tongue protruding from between swollen lips...

He was gone.

Bob's relationship with his son was not what he had considered ideal. The boy had been a disappointment, nearly from day one, and the pathetic attempts that Kyle had made to overcompensate had done more to further infuriate Bob than to charm him.

But he was still his son.

The little boy who'd cried the first time he had to bait a hook with a worm. The kid who'd ridden his bike straight into a freshly oiled patch of road, taken a nasty spill, and who, as a result, had spent a good hour or so trying not to scream as Bob had dug bits of gravel from skinned elbows and knees.

His only son.

"You dumbass," he said quietly, half-heartedly.

There was a gasp from the doorway, and Bob spun to see Sam standing there, staring.

"What the hell are you doing here?" Bob said, the surprise coming out as anger in his voice.

Sam was frozen, eyes wide, mouth agape.

"W-We saw the truck. We didn't know what was going on."

"Well," Bob said quietly, sardonically. "Now you do."

"God, Bob ... Is he...?"

"Yes."

Zachary arrived behind Sam and said, "What happened?"

"An accident. A stupid accident. We need to go downstairs. Talk this over."

Zachary glanced at Sam as they descended the stairs. She looked scared, too.

When they were in the kitchen, Bob said, "As I'm sure you can imagine, my son had problems. A lot of problems. They got much worse after his mother died. I tried to help him. Gave him a job, a home, but ... well, these days they'd say he had an addiction. A few months ago, I caught him with that ... thing. I told him to get rid of it. Obviously, he didn't. I don't know if you two know this, but another developer is in the process of buying this property. If the police come here to take a dead body out—especially one in circumstances like these—the deal will fall through."

Bob's eyes were red-rimmed. He was pale.

And, Zachary noticed for the first time, he was old.

Newly old.

"As security here, I would most likely be sued for negligence. I'd lose everything, including my reputation. And that's about the only thing I have left. Do you understand?"

Sam nodded.

"You do?" Zachary said.

"Sure. He wants to take Kyle home. Call the cops from there."

Zachary looked to Bob, who was now nodding.

"Yes, exactly. That's exactly what I want."

Zachary was incredulous. "But we can't do that."

"I'm not asking you to do a damn thing. All you have to do is go back to the office and forget about this."

Zachary shook his head. "I don't know, Bob."

"It's not like he was murdered. It's not like we're disrupting a crime scene."

Zachary remained unconvinced.

"Zach, I am asking you man to man. Please. Let me care for my son my own way. Don't let them turn him into ... into some kind of joke."

Zachary looked at Sam. She nodded slightly.

Finally, he said, "All right."

Bob let out a slow, shuddering breath. "Thank you. Thank you both. I really appreciate what you're doing for me and for Kyle. But this means I'm not going to make it in tomorrow. Zachary, would you mind coming in early? I'll pay you overtime."

"Sure, Bob," Zachary said, a sinking in his gut.

"Not to do rounds. To help Rebecca with payroll."

Zachary looked at his boss. The old man was shattered, that was true, but on some level, he had to know that he was doing Zachary a massive solid with this seemingly insignificant act. "Sure, he said. "I can do that for you. No problem." Zachary wanted to believe that he was doing what he was doing out of compassion, out of a need to help his grieving boss. And not the thought of spending hours sitting next to his work crush.

(or his first work crush, anyway)

He wanted to believe that, but deep down he knew that it wasn't the case. And while this made him feel pretty shitty about himself, that same deep, reptilian voice that cackled with glee at such an opportunity told his conscience to sit down and shut up.

"Here's the keys to my office and file cabinets. Truck key is on there, too, go ahead and take it. I'll use Kyle's Jeep to get him out of here and pick up my truck later. Computer login and password are taped to the underside of the keyboard."

Sam said, "How did you know?"

Bob said, "What?"

"About Kyle. How did you know where he was?"

"Because I put a locator app on his phone back when I bought it. Told him it was because he had a habit of losing things. Why?"

"Zachary and I thought we saw someone here last night."

"We did?"

Sam glared at him. "Yeah. Remember?"

Zachary finally understood that she was trying to see if Kyle was who Joe had seen driving the van. "Oh, yeah."

Bob frowned. "Probably that bum."

"No," Sam said. "We saw headlights. Which makes sense if Kyle was coming in here like this. But if it wasn't Kyle..."

Bob took his phone from his pocket and opened the "Lokator" app again. "What time?"

"I can't remember," Sam said.

Bob scrolled through his son's history and shook his head. "Wasn't him. According to this, he was home from 5:30 last night until 6:00 this morning."

Sam looked back at Zachary, her face serious. If the killer wasn't Kyle, then that meant they were still out there.

"I don't guess it matters much anyway," Bob muttered as he put the phone away.

"Why not?" Zachary said.

Bob looked at each of them for a moment before saying, "Because. This is the end of the line for me, guys. It'll take some time to find a new security outfit to take over, but I can't do this anymore. And I'm sorry that means that you kids will be out of a job, but I hope you can understand…"

Sam nodded. Zachary noticed that her eyes shone with tears, and he wasn't sure if she was sad for Bob or for the loss of her job. As for himself, Zachary didn't exactly know what to feel.

He didn't much like the job itself. It felt redundant and pointless to guard a bunch of abandoned houses because some rich developers were feuding over who was supposed to pay to finish the place. But Bob had been a halfway decent boss, anyway, and he liked his co-workers. Hell, he really liked some of them.

"Should I tell the others?" Zachary asked.

Bob considered this. Then, after sucking in a deep breath, he said, "Don't tell them about this. About Kyle being here, I mean. Just tell them it's a family emergency. When word gets out about Kyle's … passing, then they'll understand."

Zachary looked back toward Sam, but she was already halfway to the door. Bob was slowly climbing the stairs again, looking like a man carrying a terrible weight.

"Do you need help? With him, I mean?"

Bob stopped on the stairs. Without turning around, he said, "No. Some things a man should do alone."

Zachary nodded slowly and followed Sam to the truck.

Once they were both inside, he said, "I can't believe this."

"So much for proof of cosmic justice."

"What?"

"You heard him. That's it. We're out of a job, and the killer isn't. Now he's part of the 99% that get away with it."

Zachary stared at her. "You're giving up?"

"I'm accepting reality," she said. "You should try it. Stings a bit at first, but you'll get used to it."

"I only accept the things I can't change."

Sam laughed, but tears streaked her cheeks. "I would say this qualifies."

"I wouldn't."

"Whatever. Let's go."

She started the truck and backed out of the driveway.

On the way to the security office, they sat silently until Zachary said, "The one percent matters, you know."

"Yeah? How so?"

"Because it's proof. It shows that you can make a difference."

She looked at him. This time there was no smile, no indication of any warmth at all. "Good luck with that."

She parked, killed the engine, and got out. Without another word to him, she headed straight for her VW Bug.

"Where are you going?" he called after her.

"Home."

"What about the rest of our shift?"

"What's Bob gonna do, fire me?"

He started walking after her, trying to catch her before she got into her car. "Will I see you tomorrow?"

"Not if I find another job."

"Sam, wait!"

"Have fun playing boss," she said as she got into her car.

"And enjoy your time with Rebecca." She punctuated this by slamming the door.

Zachary stood there, staring dumbly at Sam's VW as she pulled out, kicking up dust and gravel in her hurry to leave.

"What the actual fuck?" he said.

23

After Ollie and David arrived for their shift, Zachary told them what was going on. He left out the details, of course, as Bob had asked him. But it seemed the vagueness only made them take what he said less seriously.

"Are you pranking us," David asked, eyes blazing. "Because if you are, I swear to God I'll break your ankles."

"What?" Zachary said, reflexively taking a step backward. "I'm not. It's what Bob told me to tell you."

"Why all of a sudden?" Ollie asked.

Zachary shook his head and said, "It's not that sudden, really. He's been thinking about it."

"Maybe I need to help him unthink about it."

"I told you, there's someone buying the property and he's dealing with another family emergency."

Ollie rolled his eyes. "Yeah. Kyle probably got his dick caught in his zipper."

Zachary swallowed hard and then hoped like hell that he didn't appear suspicious.

"Bob's gettin' up there in years," he said, "and with all this, well, it's a pretty perfect time for him to retire."

"Shit," David said.

"Shit is right," Ollie said. "Did he say how long we got?"

"No," Zachary said. "But two weeks is standard, isn't it?"

"Two weeks? It took me two months to find this damned job."

"I'm sorry. I'm in the same boat, man."

"No, you're not," Ollie said as he stood up, visibly pissed. "Who's gonna hire a flabby old man? Let me disabuse you of that notion right now."

"Not everybody thinks that way. Besides you're not that old. Or flabby." Zachary felt stupid even as he said it.

"Easy for you to say."

"Yeah," David agreed.

"I have to go," Zachary said. "I only stayed around to let you guys know. I'll see you in the morning."

"Don't you mean tomorrow night?"

Zachary said, "No, with everything going on, Bob's not coming in tomorrow. He asked me to come in early and help Rebecca with payroll."

"See?" David said. "Ollie's been here longer than you, but for some reason, Bob's giving you a promotion first."

"It's not a promotion. And I'm sure it's only because I was the one here when he called in."

"Course you are," David said, staring again.

Zachary felt heat rushing into his cheeks, so he turned and hurried out of the trailer before they could start giving him shit about that, too.

- 24 -

Zachary got up at 5:00 the next morning. He showered, shaved, downed a pot of coffee, and was at the office by 6:30, all part of his plan to beat Rebecca there. He wanted to look ambitious, industrious, together.

Cool.

He wanted to seem cool. Not, as appearances might lead one to believe, like a slacker with little motivation and even fewer prospects. Girls like Rebecca, he assumed, wanted to be taken care of. They wouldn't waste time with somebody who ... well, with someone like Zachary.

When she came through the trailer door at ten to 7:00, he stepped out of Bob's office as casually as he could and said, "Hey."

Rebecca frowned. "What are you doing here?" she asked. "Where's Bob?"

"Some kind of family emergency," Zachary said. "Bob asked me to fill in for him."

"Really?" she said, with a tone of disbelief that Zachary didn't much care for. Why was it so hard to think he was capable of filling in for Bob?

"Yep. That's right. So, if you wouldn't mind, why don't you put down your stuff, get settled, and then we'll get started on the payroll."

"Does this have anything to do with the sale?"

"I'm not really sure what's going on, but from what I do know, Bob is going to be looking for another security firm to take over."

"He's really going to retire?"

"Seems like. I know it's kind of a shock first thing in the morning, but I sort of figured that we could power through the payroll and then maybe spend a little time job hunting together."

She ignored his comments and only muttered to herself, "I was afraid of this."

Zachary cleared his throat and tried again. "Do you want to get started?"

She turned, and his breath caught in his throat. Her eyes were wide, bright with excitement.

"Why don't you do it?" she said.

She was so perfect it was hard to look directly at her.

When his brain finally started working again, he said, "Do what? The payroll? I mean, I've never done it before. I'm sort of supposed to help you. And, y'know, supervise."

"I'm not talking about that. I'm talking about the business. You could take it over!"

"What?"

"Bob wants to retire, right? That doesn't mean we all have to lose our jobs. He could promote you. Right? Exactly like he did for today, only permanent. Then he could run off to live on a boat in Florida or whatever, like he always said he wanted to. And you'd be in charge."

Zachary felt a strange sensation inside. It was perhaps

3/4 fear, the kind of fear that made his knees wobbly and his stomach queasy.

But the other 1/4 was something new.

It was exhilaration.

More than that, it was exhilaration that the most beautiful woman in the entire world believed in him enough to think he could do this.

And that 1/4 was enough to overpower the pants-shitting terror he felt.

Still, reality threw about 20,000 excuses in his path.

"Well," he stammered. "I mean ... that's a really interesting ... I mean ... I hadn't thought of that, honestly. But I'm not ... I don't exactly know this side of the business."

Rebecca smiled and stepped forward, putting a reassuring hand on his shoulder. "But I do! I could help with that stuff."

"You'd do that?"

"Of course! Besides, it'd be a whole lot easier to show you the ropes than it would be to go looking for a new job."

That made a certain kind of sense, he supposed, and it would be nice to work so closely with Rebecca.

"I bet everyone else would feel the same way."

"I don't know about that," he said, thinking what David and Ollie would say if he told them he was their new boss. Then he thought about Sam. About what a shit he was. He was here, thinking of only himself, and Sam was ... where? Still upset, no doubt. Still certain that a masked murderer was out there, free.

"And you know," Rebecca continued, like a host on the Home Shopping Network or something. "This could be perfect. If the sale goes through, it still takes a fairly long time to sort out all the details. Whoever buys the development, they're going to need security. I'd say we'd probably have about six months of good, on the job training to get you up to speed. By the time the development is refurbished and ready to start selling houses, you'd be way ready to take on a new contract." She smiled again, melting away all thoughts of Sam, or of masked killers, or of anything else.

He smiled back. "This could really work."

"Course it could. You're a smart guy, and I know you want more out of life than working security."

He nodded, but he was utterly lost in her eyes.

"Zachary?"

Shit. Had he been staring at her like a creeper? "Yes?"

"I said, don't you think you should call Bob and talk to him about it? Before he finds another company to take over?"

"Oh. Right."

There was a definite possibility he'd been staring at her like a creeper. Still, she didn't seem fazed.

"I'll get him on the phone for you!" she said, turning and running like a schoolgirl into her office. She bent over her desk to get the phone, and Zachary felt himself swoon a little.

No way this was real life. Must be a lucid dream, he thought.

In a lucid dream, though, he sorta doubted he'd have to actually talk to his grief-stricken boss. That part wasn't so great. Bob clearly didn't want to be on the phone. He sounded practically catatonic. But with some unspoken reassurance from Rebecca, Zachary was calm, cool, and oh so super smooth. Zachary told Bob that he only wanted what was best for everybody. He had the ability to provide a service that would make Bob's life easier. That's all.

Afterward it occurred to him that there was the slight

chance that Bob had thought Zachary was trying to black-mail him.

Zachary would never do that. But if that thought was what it took to make Bob act, well ... that was okay, right?

"I understand completely, sir. Of course. Take all the time you need and thank you again. Bye."

He hung up and turned to Rebecca.

"Well?"

"He said he'll think about it. Wants to talk more tomorrow."

"That's great!"

She was smiling at him again, this time with her head cocked slightly. Her body language seemed more ... open.

"Is it too premature to say 'congratulations'?"

"Probably," Zachary said. "Especially since we haven't even started on the payroll yet. My tenure will be cut very short if I can't complete the one task he's given me."

"Good point. Let me run to the ladies' room right quick and then we'll crank it out. It'll go faster with the two of us working together."

"Sounds great."

"Oh, and if you do take over? That is the number one thing that needs fixed. We need access to actual bathrooms, not these gross port-a-potties."

Zachary picked up a notepad and pen and wrote down her suggestion with a big "#1" beside it. He turned the pad toward her.

She laughed.

"Be right back," she said.

As soon as she left the security office, Zachary jumped out of his chair. Maybe it was the pot of coffee he'd slammed, maybe it was the craziness of the morning, maybe it was being in Rebecca's perfect aura for this long, he didn't know, but he was vibrating. He had to move. He found himself pacing around the common area, through Bob's office to gather the paperwork, then into Rebecca's office to lay out the paperwork on her desk.

And that's when he saw it:

Rebecca's Facebook page was open. And there, below the little thumbnail photos of her friends, were more little thumbnails of Rebecca herself. Including the one that had caught his eye instantly.

He looked around quickly, making absolutely certain that he was still alone. Then, before his conscience could jump in and say anything stupid, he clicked on the photo to enlarge it.

It wasn't like he was REALLY snooping, after all. These were photos any of her friends could see. And, well, he and Rebecca WERE friends, right? Zachary figured that it wouldn't be long before they'd be Facebook friends. Hell, maybe even today. And then he'd be able to click on any of these pictures and it wouldn't be at all like he was snooping, nope, just good old fashioned friendly behavi—OH. MY. GOD.

The photo had loaded. In it, a younger Rebecca stood beside an Olympic swimming pool. She was wearing a white bikini that showed off the kind of body that supermodels, porn stars, and Greek goddesses would envy. Beside her, an older man with a pencil-thin mustache stood, smiling. He had his arm around her, his hand cupping her supple, bare side.

Zachary stared in literal, actual awe, his heart pounding.

There was a sound that barely registered. The sound of the port-a-potty door, he realized.

"Shiiiiiit!" he said, quickly clicking away from the picture. In that moment of panic, he missed the little X that would return him to her profile page and instead clicked the right arrow. The photo advanced to the next photo in her "Senior Year" album. And though he quickly positioned the cursor arrow over the correct spot this time, his hand could not move.

The new photo showed Rebecca again, this time fully clothed. The expression on her face alone would've made him stop to study the photo. There was something wrong with her smile. It was too wide; her eyes were too frantic. In the photo beside her stood another older man, this one making a great show of handing her a set of keys.

"Thank you, Dad!" The caption to the photo read. "Perfect for trips to the beach!"

Behind them in the photo was her gift.

A white van.

"No," Zachary whispered. "That can't be..."

He heard her on the steps outside.

Too quickly, he clicked at the X, then stood up straight.

When Rebecca returned, she immediately knew some-thing was off. Zachary was grinning, but wouldn't look at her. And that wasn't like him. Not at all.

"Everything okay?" she asked.

"Yeah, totally. I got the paperwork and stuff from Bob's office and got it moved over to your desk. I was going to grab a chair." He slid past her, presumably to get one of the folding chairs from Bob's office.

She entered her office and sat down. She was about to open the file marked "Payroll" when she noticed that Face-book had been minimized. Which meant Zachary had been looking. She maximized the browser and saw the picture of her and her father and her white van.

"Here we go," Zachary said, bringing in the chair.

Rebecca closed the tab and said, "I haven't had any caffeine today. I'm dying for a soda. Can I get you one?"

Zachary was sitting down as she stood and grabbed her purse from the desk. "Uh ... No, I'm good. Thanks, though."

"Okay," she said, smiling.

She went into the muster room and put her purse in her locker.

"Oh, dammit. Zachary? I forgot about the stupid soda machine. Kyle always helps me with it. Could you help me?"

"I can try," Zachary said and went past her to the machine. He was about to hit the side of it when she jammed a Taser into the small of his back and keyed the trigger.

She bit her lip coquettishly as she watched him tense and writhe, the electricity seizing his muscles.

He fell, hitting the card table and flipping it before

landing on his face. She grabbed a tonfa from one of the other lockers and brought it down on his right shin, his left shin, and across his right forearm as he lifted it to protect himself. He was screaming, crying. Pathetic really.

And the sound of the tonfa—lacquered wood with a lead core—striking bone only made him louder. But that was okay. It was only the two of them today, after all. And nobody else for the next eight hours or so. They could enjoy their time alone.

She brought the baton down on the back of Zachary's skull as he tried, in vain, to crawl away.

Rebecca had gone outside, once she had the troublesome Mr. Frenkel properly subdued and secured, and backed up the Tin Star Security truck as closely as possible to the office stairs. It was a bright, clear day, and even though weeks could pass without any unexpected visitors to the development, Rebecca was a strong believer in Murphy's law and she took no chances.

Back inside, she stepped over Zachary. He was a pitiful sight: bound and gagged with duct tape, bloody, battered. She never figured him for much of a fighter anyway (he was far too much of a beta male for that) but now? He was putty in her hands.

Rebecca took a pair of walkie talkies from the muster room and went back into her office. She used a strip of duct tape to tape down the send button on one of the radios, then stashed it beneath an open binder, obscuring it from view. She turned up the volume on the other radio, then said, "Testing, testing."

The walkie talkie on her desk picked up her voice and transmitted it through the other radio clear as day. With a grin, she clipped the second radio to the waist of her skirt and returned to the break room.

Zachary was stirring ever so slightly. She could tell that it hurt him to move. She didn't think she'd whacked him hard enough to break any bones, but given the already mottled storm of bruising on his face, she imagined that his chest and legs would look quite a mess.

His eyes, so wide and white amidst that mass of bruising and blood, fixed on her even as they struggled to focus.

"There you are. I was starting to think that last shot to your temple might've put you down for good."

Zachary struggled to roll onto his side. He looked very much like a fish out of water. And like a fish out of water, it was clear he was suffering as he flopped about. "Why are you doing this?" he tried to say.

At least, she assumed that's what he was trying to say, with his mouth sealed by tape. The way he looked now, combined with that weak, barely audible voice? Rebecca had to admit that it was a bit of a turn on. But that impulse was not something she could give in to. Not something she would allow herself to feel.

She dug her fingers into her palm. Not enough to draw blood, but enough to hurt.

"Because you're making me do this, Zachary," she said. "And that's too bad, really. Because I honestly thought you were different. Not totally. But enough for me to start thinking about having a relationship with you, believe it or not. But when I saw—just now—that you looked at my private pictures without my permission, I knew I was wrong. You really are the same as the rest of them. You're another creepy perv who sees me as a piece of meat designed for one purpose. To satisfy you. Well guess what?

That's what you are now. A piece of meat designed to satisfy me. How does that feel?"

She grabbed his ankles and started pulling. Thankfully, his roar of pain was mostly muffled by the gag.

"Sounds like it hurts," Rebecca said. "And you're right. It does. It hurts when no one takes you seriously. When no one cares about your opinions. Oh, they say they do. But I'm not fooled by their pretending. I see what they're really looking at. And I know what they're really thinking. They treat me like a queen so they can use me like a whore and move on to the next piece. And even though I could feel you looking at me the same way sometimes, you were also sort of nice. And that's why I thought you were different. And I began to feel something for you. I thought that I could change you, and that it was even possible that you might change me. Do you know how hard that is for me to admit to you?"

He was staring at her blankly.

He didn't know. How could he know?

She kept dragging him toward the door.

"I used to struggle with this. I used to think it was my fault. I really did. Now I know it's your fault. You and everyone like you. You're the ones with the problem. Nothing more than cockroaches, driven to spread your filth as far and wide as possible. And once I realized that, I knew I couldn't let myself be treated like a piece of meat ever again."

She stopped at the door to recover a bit, let her heart rate slow and her breathing return to normal.

The next phase had to be done right. Getting him down those steps and into the bed of the truck needed to happen quickly, because, even in as remote a location as this godforsaken development, moving a body in broad daylight was a risky proposition.

Rebecca took her pulse quickly. Good as gold. Her cardio was on point, thanks in part to two years' worth of CrossFit classes.

She peered out the window, and, satisfied that she couldn't even see any cars on the highway at this point, decided to make her move.

She opened the door, propping it open with her own body until she got a good hold of Zachary's arms and then grunted as she shifted her weight to more or less throw him down the steps.

Zachary was awake enough to turn and take the fall on his side instead of on his face. She'd learned the hard way that people were basically a bunch of liars and fakes and phonies. Every single time they pulled this crap, playing dead.

Unbelievable.

She skipped down the steps, took Zachary by the tape that bound his arms behind his back, and lifted.

This was another trick she'd learned along the way: pain, applied appropriately, was a magnificent force multiplier. She'd made men lie down in their own graves, happily, just to avoid a little pinch in their wrists or elbows or knees. Pathetic. They didn't know what pain was.

Zachary was no different, fighting to get to his feet, even on swollen and battered legs, just to ease the ache in his shoulders. A little more pressure was all it took to make him plant his face into the bed of the truck. She took his legs and lifted them, moving aside nimbly when Zachary's feet swung in her direction. Had that been intentional? Maybe. Maybe not. She never took it personally. It was merely another predictable element of this game. They all claimed to love her, but they always tried to hurt her in the end.

With Zachary safely stowed in the bed of the truck, she draped a tarp over his prone form, closed the tailgate, and returned to the office to close the door. She happened to notice a smear of blood on the break room floor and stooped to wipe it away with a paper towel before returning to the truck.

She got in and started the engine. There was no sound from the back. She imagined he was recovering from the ordeal and that was fine. She hated the part with the crying and the begging.

Looking up, she caught sight of herself in the rearview mirror, saw tears welling in her own eyes, and looked quickly away.

That wasn't her.

Not anymore.

(Not ever.)

As she drove, Rebecca admired once again how perfect it all was. She remembered the first time she'd seen Shadow Vista and how she'd immediately known that it would serve her purposes in a way that nothing else could.

The first part of her plan had required getting a job with Tin Star. But Bob already had a secretary. Shelly. That's what Bob had told her when she'd come in to apply. Rebecca had dressed appropriately that day (of course) and she could see clearly that Bob was interested in her resume, so to speak.

Rebecca chuckled to herself and thought about poor Shelly. How she'd followed her home that very night. How she'd made her write a suicide note and wash down a bottle of pills with a bottle of wine. Then she'd gone home to wait for her phone to ring. Bob had called less than 24 hours later. He'd hired Rebecca before Shelly was even in the ground. And once she got the job, she'd started looking for all the places she could use to make people disappear. That's why she'd wanted Zachary to take over. Because she wasn't even close to done yet.

At the house on Breton Road, Rebecca backed into the driveway and got out. After she found her overalls in the garage where she'd left them, she took her skirt off and put them on, then brought the wheelbarrow to the truck and lowered the tailgate. She pulled Zachary into it and started wheeling him into the backyard, talking as they went.

"I know you think you're the victim in this situation. But you're not. I am. Of genetics, for one thing. And of the stupid standards in our sick culture that say I'm beautiful. And I'm sure you think looking like I do makes things easier for me. It does not. It's a curse, Zachary. Beauty is a terrible curse. It makes things much, much harder. And it's really important to me that you understand this."

It was clear from the way he was trying to scream (and turning purple from the effort) that he did not understand what she was saying at all. She considered knocking him out again, but thought better of it. There was still a chance he would see the light. She didn't want to deny him that. More importantly, she didn't want to deny herself that.

She didn't enjoy this. She needed it.

That thought—that particular phrase—froze her in her tracks. All at once, she felt the familiar ache, deep in her shoulders, in the sockets. Arms stretched and quivering, wrists bound with rope. Usually he wrapped it around the trunk of a tree and then pulled, slow but steady, until she thought her arms might come off. Until she wished they would because that would have put an end to it.

To all of it.

And while she ached, those men smiled. Looking at her like that and they smiled.

Daddy always put something, a rolled-up towel maybe or her own dress, under her head. A small kindness. Even with everything else, there was that small, simple thing.

He didn't enjoy this. But he needed it.

They all did. And they told her she did, too.

She would work harder next time.

Better grades, better manners.

She would do better, be better.

She would swim faster.

And she did. She did it all.

But it never stopped.

The rope. The ache.

Those eyes on her. All those eyes.

She caressed the ridged edge of the utility knife in her pocket.

"You're lucky, you know?" she said quietly to Zachary. She saw his eyelids flutter. "I'll make it quicker for you."

Not quick, no. That couldn't be. But quicker, sure. That she could do. That was a kindness. A small, simple thing.

She looked down at him, at his fluttering eyes, the taut cables of muscle in his jaw and throat that told her he was hurting.

Or he thought he was.

String you up, she thought. Spread you out. See how you like that. How any of you would like that.

Look at you. Leer at you. At all of you.

Think you know what pain is.

But Zachary would never wake up in the cold room.

Alone.

Really alone, now.

No men. Not even their cameras. Not anymore.

No Daddy.

And for all that he looked at you once, he never looked at you again, did he? Only at the floor. Until you made sure he never looked at anything ever again.

No little baby, not anymore.

They paid someone to scrape her away, didn't they? To suck her out of you? And would she have a grave? Never. Not even the smallest of kindnesses. Not for her. How would she rest her little head? And it wasn't even her fault. It was—

Theirs?

...Yours?

Mistakes were made, Daddy said, but he never said who had made them.

The world snapped back into focus because Rebecca thought she saw movement out of the corner of her eye. She turned and looked but saw nothing. There was only the neighboring house, the one the builders would have to fix up before the development could even think about selling any houses. That house had broken windows. Just like her.

She looked down again at Zachary. He was looking at her now. Eyes wide again. Bloodshot and terrible.

Thrilling in a way she didn't like to think about.

"Do you know how many are here? I don't mean only this yard. I mean, like, altogether. Do you know? I don't. I know it started with Shelly. She was Bob's first receptionist. That was how I got the job. It was so much easier back then."

It would be easy to get carried away again. To get all wistful about it all.

But she looked back down at Zachary and said, "You know I really did want you to take it over. My work isn't done yet. You would have made things easier for me."

She couldn't afford to get emotional. She got control over herself and said, "It's all right. You'll be in good company here."

She pushed the wheelbarrow toward a finished area of

the patio. There was a raised firepit surrounded by cement benches.

Gesturing toward the first bench, she said, "Daddy is in that one." Pointing at the next, she said, "Over there is my swim coach."

She stopped, finger pointed at the last bench. "And that one ... I-I don't remember who's in that one. But the one thing you can count on is that they deserve to be there."

She wheeled Zachary over to another, uncompleted bench.

"And this one? I've been saving this one for someone special. And guess who that is?"

Zachary's eyes were rolling in a kind of wild, animal panic.

"That's right. It's you, Zachary."

She tipped the wheelbarrow, spilling Zachary's limp form into the narrow, coffin-like space. It was a tight fit, and she saw that he hit his elbows and shins on the concrete edges. His face went white, muscles tight in a pained wince.

Poor baby. But it was nearly over for him.

Nearly.

She walked back to the garage to get the things she needed. But the bucket she used to mix the concrete was missing, as was the trowel.

She frowned. Then she remembered the last time she'd brought someone here. The night with the children.

That had been unfortunate.

Still, it was better that they'd met a relatively painless end through her.

Life could be far crueler.

She glanced back at Zachary. Between the duct tape and the tight quarters of his soon-to-be resting place, he wasn't going anywhere.

"I'm sorry Zachary, dear. I left some things at another house. I'm afraid we can't finish without them. Don't try to go anywhere, you'll only make things worse for yourself. I'll be back in a jiffy."

- **28** -

There was a very still voice deep in the back of Zachary's mind that was trying to tell the rest of him to stay calm. To stop hyperventilating, breathe slow and deep, and start using his head.

He could get out of this, right?

But the rest of him, every primordial and animal instinct, only knew how to panic. With the duct tape over his mouth, he felt like he was slowly suffocating. He couldn't catch his breath. And breathing hurt too much anyway.

The pain was unlike anything he'd ever experienced in what he now knew had been a mercifully privileged life.

This pain was a living being, a thing that that had wrapped him in its clutches and wouldn't let him go.

He couldn't move without it squeezing him, crushing him.

His own breath, ragged in his ears, and his heartbeat—too fast, too hard—thrummed together so loudly that he thought he imagined the voice.

"Hello?"

Zachary held his breath and tried to listen over the sound of his heart. It had to be real. Had to. Someone had to be there to rescue him. It wasn't an awful trick of his pain-ravaged brain ... was it?

"Zachary?"

No, he heard it that time. Really heard it.

Unless he was going crazy, a possibility he had to admit wasn't that far-fetched.

Zachary made as much noise as he possibly could, which wasn't much. He half hummed, half screamed, and the bulk of the sound came through his most-likely-broken nose, expelling a mixture of blood, tears, and snot down his chin.

Embarrassment could come later, though.

He'd gladly be embarrassed and alive instead of blissfully shame-free but deader than shit.

A face peered over the edge of the bench. Old, scraggly, somewhat dirty. The most beautiful face he'd ever seen.

Joe.

"Holy shit, Zachary! Damn, boy. I don't even wanna know what you did to piss her off enough to do this..."

Despite the pain, which flared white hot every time he moved, Zachary flopped like a fish, trying to sit up, and held out his bound wrists. Joe leaned down to tear off the duct tape that covered Zachary's mouth, but quickly discovered that Rebecca had wound it all the way around his head. The tape was inextricably attached to Zachary's hair in a way that would not be easy to remove.

"Gonna have to cut this shit off you. You got a knife anywhere?"

Zachary tried to answer, but the tape ensured that he could only emit a muffled hum. He opened and closed his right hand and pointed down.

"In your pocket?"

Zachary nodded and attempted to turn over to give Joe access, but he couldn't move much. It didn't stop Joe. He dug into Zachary's pocket and pulled out an old pen, a coin purse, and a tape measure.

"Shit, boy, you got yourself about every damn thing but a knife."

Zachary wiggled his hand again and signaled the same pocket. Joe tried again but the result was the same.

Whatever had happened to his pocketknife, it wasn't here in his pants.

Joe took a different tact. He straddled the narrow bench and reached down, gripping him under the arms and struggling to lift him from his prison. But Joe was old, and Zachary could tell that the effort pained him. He also hadn't realized that Joe's leg was snagged on a jagged bit of rebar that peeked out from the concrete bench.

Then they both heard the truck.

Without a word, Joe dropped Zachary and ran.

Zachary's stomach sank and he felt tears in his eyes. He wouldn't have expected Joe to stand his ground and fight for him, but he also didn't know how the old man could leave him so quickly.

He struggled to control his breathing, again, against the dawning horror that he was about to die.

29

Rebecca turned the corner to the backyard and found Zachary where she'd left him, more or less. She was sure that he'd made an attempt to escape, they all did. But he didn't have the leverage to maneuver his way out of the narrow space. And it looked like he'd cut his leg a bit on some of the rebar she'd used as reinforcement.

She looked down at him staring up at her, still in disbelief. She took the utility knife from the pocket of her overalls and cut open the bag of cement.

He was still watching as she dumped some of the powder into the wheelbarrow. She used a bucket she'd brought with her to get water from a rain barrel near the fence.

With the trowel, she mixed the powder and water until it was the correct consistency.

And still Zachary watched her.

His eyes were always on her. Had always been on her.

But the knife in her pocket would fix that. She felt for it and realized that it wasn't in her pocket. She must've left it—

Zachary wasn't looking at her anymore. He was looking behind her.

She turned, saw the old man, the bum, and her knife in his hand. He'd been quiet, she had to give him that.

Without a thought, she took the half empty bag of cement and swung it, striking the old man in the chest, knocking him into one of the finished benches.

The bench hit him right behind the knees, taking his balance, and he fell, almost comically, backward. She half-expected the old bastard to break his neck, but he knew how to take a fall.

She grabbed the shovel from the ground near her feet and lifted it overhead, swinging it down like an axe aimed directly at the bum's face.

At the last second, he rolled, and the impact of the shovel against the concrete sent numbing shockwaves up the handle and into the bones of Rebecca's hands.

He was up again and slashing at her with the knife.

Instinct took over, and she moved the shovel handle sideways, striking his wrist in such a way that the utility knife spun out of his hand. The old man winced and held his arm close to his body, turning on his heels as if to run away.

Rebecca wondered if she were strong enough—and he feeble enough—that she could put the shovel blade through his spine. She cocked her arm back, willing to give it a shot, anyway, when the bum fell to his knees in front of her.

Fair enough, she thought, she'd put it through his neck instead.

He turned, and too late, she realized his ruse. He had a handful of dirt and sand and concrete powder from the ground, and before she could raise a hand to block it, it was in her face.

She dropped the shovel, frantically wiping at her eyes, fearful that the concrete might mix with her tears.

She'd cleared enough of it away to see the old man, head lowered like a bull, charging at her midsection.

That technique would surely have worked for him 40 years ago, when he was young and quick and thick with muscle. Now, though, she was the quick one. She took a step to the side, trailing her right foot to let it hook his ankle.

The old bum went sprawling.

She stooped to retrieve her shovel and, by the time she had it, the old bastard was back on his hands and knees.

She swung the shovel like a golf club, the flat edge breaking his nose and rocketing his head back.

Whether he was dead or unconscious didn't matter to her at the moment. She used her sleeve to wipe her eyes. Then, satisfied that the bum wasn't moving, returned to her previous task.

"Sorry, Zachary. It's you and me alone again."

The look on his face was priceless.

All hope was gone.

He closed his eyes.

"Hello?"

Rebecca's entire body sagged. "You've gotta be fucking kidding me," she hissed.

The voice, female and familiar over the radio, called out again.

Rebecca turned to Zachary, sighed, and shrugged before getting back in the truck to start driving, quite fast, toward the security office.

30

Sam stood in the middle of the reception area. The place was deserted, even though both Zachary's Camry and Rebecca's Civic were in the lot. Which struck her as more than a little odd. It wasn't like they'd go on rounds together. Even if there was an issue on the property, Zachary wouldn't take Rebecca. She wasn't security.

She'd checked both offices and now moved into the muster room. Sam's locker was open. In it, her spare uniform hung from a hook, and a photocopy of an old picture of her and her dad was taped to the inside of the door.

But what stood out to her was what wasn't there. Her tonfa, stun gun, and radio were missing.

She checked the other lockers (her co-workers didn't bother actually putting locks on the doors because the development was such a ghost town nobody worried about theft) and saw that several radios were missing. She finally found Ollie's walkie talkie, turned it on, and depressed the send button as she returned to the reception area.

"Zachary? It's Sam. Do you read me? Where in hell are you?"

She took her thumb off the button and winced as the radio in her hand squealed with feedback. She reflexively moved it away from her ear, and the pitch and volume of the noise changed.

She froze and turned, instinctively using the radio in her hand like a Geiger counter, moving around the room, listening for the worst feedback. She stopped in front of the door to Rebecca's office, then stepped inside. It didn't take her long to find the radio concealed beneath the opened binder on Rebecca's desk, or to frown at the tape holding the talk button down. She turned Rebecca's radio off and ran back to the muster room.

Sam wasn't in uniform—she'd worn an old tie-dyed shirt and a pair of jeans—and she was aware that strapping on her duty belt would look a bit conspicuous, but she wanted access to her weaponry, so she did it anyway, pulling her t-shirt over it as best as she could.

She was on her way outside, thinking that she'd do a quick scan of the property by car and see if she spotted anything weird, when she saw the Tin Star Security truck speeding toward the office from inside Shadow Vista.

Sam ducked back inside, out of sight, and locked the door. Then, second guessing herself, she reached up and unlocked it.

She pulled her tonfa from her belt, considered what she was doing, then slipped it back again.

Pepper spray. She'd settle for the pepper spray. She took it in a hand that trembled and crouched behind Rebecca's desk.

Part of what was fucking with her head, she realized as she crouched beneath the desk, was that, for all her training, she didn't have a good feel for what real violence was like. It wasn't something that martial arts classes—even "full contact"—could teach, because the very context let you know that it wasn't real fighting, only practice.

She didn't know who was in the truck. But if Rebecca came through that door...

What if everything Sam had pieced together was nothing more than conspiracy theory and panic and (jealousy) ... and nonsense? What if Rebecca wasn't as guilty as Sam believed she was?

When was the precise moment, the right moment, to physically attack another human being? In law enforcement, and in most martial arts training, she was taught to wait until she'd already been attacked.

Well, duh, that was a sign you could fight back, sure.

But what if that first attack was something she wasn't able to defend against? What if Rebecca had a gun? Against Sam's pepper spray? Wouldn't it be better to strike first and apologize later if she was wrong?

But the idea of lawsuits and news stories and social media swam through Sam's mind. And yes, as her father used to say, it was better to be judged by 12 than carried by six, but that wasn't the way of the world anymore. She would be, in the public's eyes, guilty. Crazy.

The arguments whirling through Sam's mind at 90 MPH came to an abrupt end when Rebecca strolled into the office.

31

Rebecca didn't look as put together as usual, though. Her skirt was a wrinkled mess. Her blouse, too. It had come untucked in places. Her cheeks were rosy, her face looked ... dirty? And her hair was mussed, though it was clear she'd tried to tie it up into a neat ponytail.

"Sam?" Rebecca called out, looking around the office.

"Stop!" Sam found herself saying. She was still crouched, but she had the pepper spray ready and aimed.

Rebecca looked at her with a mix of amusement and horror, unable to decide if Sam was being serious.

"God, Sam, you scared the shit out of me. What's going on? What are you doing with that pepper spray?"

"Where's Zachary?"

Rebecca stopped moving.

"I don't know. He said he was going to check something on the property, and that he'd be right back. That was over an hour ago. I tried calling him on the radio, but when he didn't respond, I took the truck and went looking for him. That's why I rigged that radio. I thought if he came back, I'd hear him … I thought maybe his radio malfunctioned or something."

Throughout Sam's life, she'd learned that she was not a natural born poker player. Her face tended to betray whatever was going on in her head, and right now she could tell from Rebecca's reaction that her skepticism was on full display.

Rebecca took another step forward. "What are you doing here anyway? You're not scheduled until 3:00 and you're not really supposed to be in my office."

"I needed to tell Zachary something," Sam said. Her voice sounded far steadier than she felt. Thank God for small favors.

"Why didn't you call him?"

"Because I was worried he might be in danger. And apparently I was right."

Rebecca looked confused and then laughed.

Sam took her cell phone out of her pocket and started to dial.

"Yes! Call him. I'm sure he's got his phone."

Sam shook her head. "I'm calling the cops."

Rebecca started to close the gap between them but stopped when Sam raised the pepper spray.

"Don't! Okay? Just don't. Fuck. I'll explain, okay?"

Sam's thumb froze over the send button on her phone.

"I'm listening."

"I lied, all right? He's not missing. I know exactly where he is." She sighed, and Sam noticed that she looked very flushed.

"And?" Sam said. "Where is he?"

Rebecca looked at the floor, suddenly uncomfortable.

"He's … back at one of the houses. Waiting for me. We heard you on the radio and, um, thought that one of us should come and talk to you. Because neither of us wanted you to find out this way. I'm really sorry."

"Find out what?"

"Well ..." Rebecca said. "I mean ... We've been kinda talking a lot lately ... and we sorta hit it off, y'know? And then today? With nobody else around? I mean, I don't think either of us intended for anything to happen ... but it did."

Sam stared at her. At her disheveled clothes and her mussed hair. Something small and hot and sick coiled in her gut. "Bullshit."

"Oh, c'mon, Sam. I know you guys are friends. He never talked about me? You never noticed the way he looks at me?"

Sam's jaw was tight, and her breath was in her throat. "Okay," Sam said. "Get him on the phone. I want to hear it from him."

Rebecca's face softened into a mask of pity. "Sam..."

"Do it or I call the cops."

"And tell them what? To arrest me for 'stealing' your crush?"

"No. For killing him. He's dead, isn't he?"

Rebecca opened her mouth in shock. "What? Why would you even say such a thing?"

"Because I've been reading about you on the internet. About how many people around you have ended up dead or missing."

"Sam, please," Rebecca said, taking another step closer, hands up now, trying to placate Sam. "I'm not the only Rebecca Summers, you know."

Sam felt tears in her eyes.

But not of sadness.

The hot tears of anger.

"Fuck it," she said, then pressed the dial button on her phone. "I'll let the police figure it out."

In a millisecond, the woman before her changed. Even disheveled and dirty, Rebecca Summers was one of the most beautiful women Sam had ever seen. She exuded that kind of effortless perfection that A-list movie stars did.

That wasn't the creature that leapt at her now, fingers like claws outstretched, eyes bulging, strings of saliva hanging from a red, open mouth. That thing slapped the phone out of Sam's hand like she was swatting a fly. It bounced off the desk and hit the wall with enough force to shatter the case.

Sam tensed, triggering the pepper spray, and it fired directly into Rebecca's horrid face for an instant before the woman's grip closed on Sam's wrist, wrenching it back. The pepper spray continued to spray, up toward the ceiling, after which it rained down on both of them.

Sam pulled her shirt over her nose and mouth, which may have helped a tiny bit, but the effects of the spray still hit her hard.

Her eyes were burning so intensely she couldn't see through the tears, and she was coughing hard enough to retch. She could hear her murderous co-worker gasping for air. In between wracking gasps, she rasped, "You. Fucking. Bitch. You're. Dead. You're. Fucking. Dead."

She heard the door slam and, seconds later, the truck starting.

Sam felt around for her phone. Finding it in pieces, she cursed to herself and moved into the fresher air of the reception area.

She took a half-empty bottled water from Bob's desk, threw her head back, and poured it into her eyes. It helped a little, though her vision was still blurry, and it hurt to breathe.

"Fuck!" she screamed.

Her first instinct when Rebecca left was that she was escaping.

But what if she wasn't?

What if Zachary was alive and she was going back to him?

What if she—?

Sam turned and was halfway to the door when she heard the truck's engine rev.

Rebecca hadn't left?

But then what was she—?

Sam heard the truck's wheels squeal. Then, with horrifying clarity, she knew exactly what the crazy bitch was doing. Sam turned, running toward Bob's office, when the Tin Star Security truck slammed into the office, knocking the trailer off its simple post-and-block foundation. The entire trailer tipped and, as the wood and metal screamed, Sam fell and slid through the reception area, colliding with the muster room's door frame.

She was wobbly and everything hurt, but she knew she needed to get out. Even though the front door was only five feet away, with the floor slanting at such a steep angle, and nothing to hold onto, it may as well have been five miles.

She heard the truck engine revving again, partially saw it through the cracked window in the reception area as it backed up, pulling ribbons of vinyl skirting with it.

Behind the wheel, Rebecca looked truly insane. Her hair was a nimbus of fire around her head. The skin around her eyes was an angry red from the pepper spray, and her lips were pulled back, showing what seemed to Sam like too many teeth, bared in a rictus of pain and rage and triumph.

Because she was preparing to ram the office again.

She's really going to kill me, Sam thought.

Rapidly changing strategy, Sam turned and ran down the sloping floor toward the back of the temporary building. In Rebecca's office, she took the psycho's desktop computer and heaved it through the window, using the keyboard to clear any stray shards of glass before climbing out.

She had made it nearly half through the window when the truck slammed into the building again.

If Sam had begun climbing through the window even a second later, or the truck had rammed the building a second earlier, Sam realized, the impact may have cut her in half. As it was, the kinetic energy threw her clear of the window, which crumpled as the rear wall collapsed.

Through the exhaustion, the pain, and an almost paralyzing fear, Sam got up.

And she ran.

32

A fresh cut had opened above Rebecca's left eye. She absent-mindedly wiped away the blood and saw Sam running. Toward the development.

Convenient.

Maybe she'd run herself right into her own grave.

Rebecca shifted into reverse and gunned the engine, but nothing happened.

She frowned and got out. The mangled front steps had buckled down over the bumper.

The scream of frustration that erupted from Rebecca's lungs was so feral in its intensity that it frightened even her.

A little.

But it was also sort of nice to let it all out.

And what she was finding, what she always suspected in the deepest recesses of her heart, was that the wellspring of rage within her was inexhaustible.

That unleashing it, as she had, only increased the thirst to unleash even more, without ever depleting the supply.

Rebecca glanced back at Sam's silhouette fleeing into the distance and grunted as she took her overalls from beneath the tarp in the bed of the truck. She'd pulled them on over her office clothes before, in her hurry to get to work on Zachary. Then she'd taken them off to face Sam.

Now she had to put them back on.

Thankful there were no eyes here, she stripped in the middle of the parking lot, throwing the ruined blouse and skirt on the pavement near the demolished office. The breeze cooled her irritated skin but did little against the fire of shame she felt welling up again.

"No," she said out loud. That shame wasn't hers. It was theirs. It belonged to all of them, not to her.

She slipped into the overalls and pulled on her heavy boots. Once they were laced tightly, she climbed onto the hood of the truck and unleashed more of that limitless rage, bouncing up and down, stomping the shame down, ignoring the pain. Finally, the metal relented and the bumper popped free of the collapsed stairs with a hollow clang.

Rebecca smiled to herself and wiped a stray strand of hair out of her eyes.

Back in the truck, she gunned it once more and whooped in triumph as the truck careened into a U-turn.

Sam was at the front gate of the property when she heard it. Turning from the lock and chain, she saw the truck, saw Rebecca, coming for her.

She yanked the chain free, opened the gate far enough to slip through, then pulled it closed behind her, wrapped the chain around the support poles, snapped the lock in place, and dove out of the way.

Part of her expected it to be like the movies, the truck hitting the fence and smashing through.

But that wasn't what happened.

The fence was strong, and the lock did not snap. Instead, everything bent inward like a net. Sam smiled in disbelief. But she was all too aware that her luck could run out at any time. She got up, turned toward Katz Parkway, and ran.

Rebecca scowled at her through the gate, then switched off the truck's ignition and climbed out.

Matching the padlock on the gate to the right key on the ring, she snapped it open and yanked the chain free. But when she tried to open the gate, she saw it was too bent, too twisted, to function properly.

Instead of screaming, she smiled.

Sam and Zachary and the old man were in her kingdom now. At the same time, she realized something that she had not in her impatience: it was far easier for Rebecca to get in than it would be for them to get out.

She dropped the chain and lock to the ground, then got into the truck, started it, and drove toward the northwest corner.

Inside, Sam ran, though she'd fallen into a sort of loping, limping skip now that her ankle had swollen. She called out, hoping to hear from Zachary, or from Joe (if he was still around).

The houses loomed around her, silent, still things. They may as well have been tombstones.

Sam thought about the area where they'd found the shoe and she turned west toward that section of the development.

She heard Rebecca's truck before she saw it, but there it was, racing by, still outside the fence, but coming her way. Sam turned, running in the opposite direction and weaving through the vacant yards, slipping behind peeling picket fences to avoid being seen.

33

Zachary wasn't sure if he'd lost consciousness or if he'd gone into shock, but he was suddenly awake. He heard a violent coughing nearby.

Then, Joe's voice: "Fuck me! I ain't felt this shitty since '72."

Zachary gathered his energy and screamed as hard as the tape gag allowed. The pressure made his head feel like it was going to burst, but he still made enough noise to attract the old man.

"Hold on, buddy. I'm comin'. Hope you didn't think I'd leave you hangin' like this. Let's get you out of there."

Joe's face appeared in Zachary's field of vision and he immediately saw the knife. His knife. The old guy must've found the thing on the ground. And for the first time in what felt like an eternity, Zachary felt hope swelling inside him.

Joe cut the tape that bound Zachary's wrists, then the strips that had bound his upper arms to his chest. As soon as one arm was free, Zachary struggled to pull himself upright. The blood returned, bringing a thousand needle pricks to dance along his muscles. But he didn't care. That was a good sort of pain, he supposed. He hefted himself again.

"Wait, partner!" Joe said, but Zachary didn't wait. He had to get the fuck out of that bench. Joe tried to help but Zachary's leg slipped free of the jagged rebar and he flipped over the side of the cement bench and landed on the ground hard enough to knock the wind out of his lungs.

Rolling over, Zachary motioned to Joe for the knife. The old man gave it to him, and Zachary went to work, freeing his ankles and then carefully cutting a strip away to unseal his mouth.

Those first unrestricted breaths were enough to make him lightheaded. He laid back, savoring the simple act of breathing, for as long as he dared to.

"We gotta get out of here. She'll be back."

He remembered the voice on the radio.

"Shit! Sam! She went after Sam!"

The panic and horror on Joe's face mirrored the way he felt.

"We have to find her!" Joe said.

Zachary got to his feet unsteadily. The pins and needles poked his legs, so he beat at the muscles with his hands to work some life back into them.

"You gonna be okay?" Joe said.

"Thanks to you," Zachary said, and noticed that Joe was beaming with pride. It made him look younger, more vital.

"C'mon," Zachary said. "We gotta move." He took several unsteady steps. As the circulation returned to his legs, so did the searing pain in his shins from where that crazy bitch had beat him.

They made it to the street, and Zachary was moving better, faster, when he saw the Tin Star Security truck pull up to the area of fencing that Kyle had attempted to repair. The truck lurched forward, breaching the fence easily.

"We gotta split up," Joe said. "If we stick together, I'll slow you down."

"That's crazy!"

"No," Joe said. "I'll hide. It's what I'm good at."

Zachary nodded and clapped the old man on the shoulder, then he half-jogged, half-limped across the street, out of sight of the truck. By the time he looked back to where Joe had been, the old man had already vanished.

– 34 –

Zachary heard the truck engine revving but couldn't tell which direction the sound was coming from. Sound had a weird way of bouncing around the empty neighborhood.

Knowing where Rebecca had entered the fence, though, gave him some indication of where she could be and where she couldn't be, and he made a quick left turn onto Lemon Tree Lane, sticking close to the houses. As he turned, a figure appeared in his peripheral vision to his right. Sam! She saw him, too, and nearly sobbed with what he assumed was relief.

She was clearly hurt. And although he had injuries of his own, he knew they stood a better chance together. He started to run in his odd, limping way to her. She, too, started running toward him. They both stopped dead in their tracks when the Tin Star truck roared into the inter-section between them and skidded to a halt.

From behind the wheel, Rebecca looked at Sam, ten yards to her right, then at Zachary, ten yards to her left. When their eyes met, he couldn't believe it was the same woman. She didn't look like a fantasy anymore. Her outer appearance now matched what Zachary knew of her inner self. She was a nightmare.

Rings of inflamed red encircled bloodshot eyes, and her mascara had run down her cheeks. Her lipstick was a bloody smear across the lower half of her face, and her teeth seemed perpetually bared.

Zachary had to admit that he wasn't particularly enamored with her anymore.

Sam screamed, "What now?"

Zachary's mind raced. Then it occurred to him.

"Meet me at Kyle's house," he yelled, figuring Sam would understand exactly what he meant and that Rebecca would have no idea what he was talking about.

Almost immediately, Sam ran, juking to the right, down Lemon Tree Lane. That wasn't the way, but Zachary assumed she did it to lead Rebecca in the wrong direction if she followed her, a trick he was ashamed to admit he hadn't thought of.

Rebecca watched Sam run for a two-count, then cranked the wheel toward Zachary and gunned the engine.

Zachary ran.

When he heard the truck closing in, he stopped to stand behind a metal streetlight pole. The truck roared past him and drove onto the unfinished lawns to swerve into a U-turn.

Zachary started running again, in the opposite direction. His legs felt very weak. The area on his calf that had been torn open by the exposed rebar felt tight and hot. He found it hard to put his full weight on that foot. Still, his concern for Sam outweighed the momentary pain. And if his muscles wouldn't do the work, he'd have to rely on will.

Strangely, to him anyway, that was enough.

Gritting his teeth, he pushed himself, and poured on all

the speed he could to cut between the houses where the truck couldn't go. After he heard it pass by, he cut back through another yard and ran to 7237 Katz Parkway.

As he reached the house, the front door opened. He felt a jolt of fear until he saw Sam's face—her sweet, beautiful, not at all psychotic face—smiling at him with that same look of relief that he'd seen before.

She closed the door as soon as he crossed the threshold. He nearly collapsed, but she caught him, squeezing him tightly until he realized how out of breath he really was.

And then her lips were on his. And he could taste blood and sweat—hers or his, he didn't know—but none of that mattered. He could breathe later.

For now, there was this. Only this.

After hours of pain, her touch was tender, sweet, and pure.

The feel and the taste and the smell of her was almost enough to make him cry, but he felt like a big enough wuss as it was.

"Sam," he said, breaking away.

"I thought you were dead," she said.

"Me too," he said. "And we may still be if we don't get the hell out of here."

"I called the cops."

A tiny flutter of hope.

"You did?"

"I ... think."

Zachary gave her a look. She said, "I had dialed 911 but then Rebecca knocked the phone out of my hand ... and it broke on the floor."

"Okay ... but you talked to the operator."

She shook her head.

Okay. That was still okay, right? Didn't they have the

ability to track phones now? They did, right? He was sure he'd heard that somewhere. And it wasn't like the movies, was it? Where they had to keep you on the line for some arbitrary amount of time in order to "trace" the call?

Or was it?

Fuck.

"How long ago?"

Sam shook her head, tears in her eyes. "I don't know. Maybe ten minutes ago."

Zachary nodded. "Let's wait upstairs." He took her hand, but she didn't move.

"I don't want to go up there."

"Why not?"

She looked at him seriously. "Because I watch horror movies. You never run upstairs in a horror movie."

"But we'd have a better vantage point. Maybe we can see where she is."

Sam shook her head and said, "You go. Keep watch. I'll stay here and do the same."

Zachary hesitated for a moment, then, having gathered his courage, leaned in and kissed Sam. It was a clumsy kiss, all mashed lips colliding with teeth, but that was all right. This was a stolen moment, a tiny bit of tenderness snatched from the jaws of fear. They were in danger, and they knew that, but they also knew that they were together.

Zachary ran up the stairs as best he could, though his muscles still ached and his injuries screamed at him. He ducked into the first bedroom and peeked out the window. The street was clear on that side of the house.

Leaving the room, he crossed the hall to the bedroom on the opposite side. He moved to the window and looked out.

Clear.

Wait...

He saw the Tin Star Security truck, parked, half-concealed behind a dumpster one street over. It was empty.

Zachary ran back to the top of the stairs and said, "Sam! You locked the doors, right?"

There was no reply.

He limped down the stairs, wincing with each step, until he stopped to take a breath at the landing.

"Sam, we might have some trouble…"

Sam came around the corner.

First, Zachary saw her face, then the Taser.

Then the hideous creature that had its arm around Sam's neck, holding the Taser to her chest.

"That's me," the bloody, crazed thing that used to be Rebecca said. "Trouble with a capital T."

- 35 -

Zachary's mind raced, trying to figure out how it was possible that Rebecca could be here, inside the house. Then it dawned on him. "You killed Kyle," he said.

Rebecca smiled. "And the world's a better place for it. Now I need your help to wrap this up."

Zachary tried to think while he surveyed the area for anything that might help them, but there was nothing. To keep Rebecca busy, he said, "So, what's your big plan here, Rebecca? You're going to somehow overpower both of us, kill us, and then hide our bodies, all while you're clearly hurt, yourself? Why can't we end this? You could leave us, make a run for it. We don't have any way to call the police."

Rebecca grinned. "In that case, I could kill you both and leave the bodies to rot. You're not thinking things through, Zachary."

"You don't have to keep hurting people," Zachary said.

The smile faded from Rebecca's face. "You don't know that."

"I do. Up until today, I thought you were a nice person.

You were a person that I liked. You could be that person. You don't have to do this—"

"You think I want this, Zachary? They put this in me."

Zachary had no idea what that meant, but he said, "What you do right now is about you, not anybody else. I'm sorry if someone hurt you, but that doesn't give you the right to hurt anyone else."

He saw the door from the garage slowly open. Joe crept in soundlessly, a shovel in his hand.

Rebecca looked confused, and her eyes filled with tears. "You don't know what they did."

"You're right," he said. "I don't. And whatever they did? They shouldn't have. Obviously. But you can't control any of that. That's in the past. You can only control what you do next."

Joe was behind her now, holding the shovel with both hands. When he was close enough to smack the back of Rebecca's head with it, he swung, but the blade struck the low ceiling with a dull clang and bounced back.

Rebecca spun, and in doing so lost her grip on Sam. Sam hit the floor and turned, scissoring her legs around Rebecca's ankles. A heartbeat later, Zachary slammed into Rebecca's back, knocking her to the carpet. He had both hands on Rebecca's wrists, keeping her from pressing the Taser into him, but he wasn't expecting her to lunge forward, closing her jaws on his forearm. He screamed and let go, balling a fist to dislodge her from his arm. In that instant, though, she pushed with unexpected strength and brought the contacts of the Taser to Zachary's bare throat.

There was only a fraction of a second of agony, though. The contact was broken almost immediately. Zachary's head lolled to the side and he saw that Sam had Rebecca in a full nelson. And though the wrestling hold had her immobilized for the time being, Rebecca was already flailing, trying to use the Taser on Sam.

Zachary saw Sam brace herself, and then she screamed, "Joe!"

The old man seemed to wake from his shock.

"Help!" Sam screamed.

Joe tightened his grip on the shovel's handle, cocked it back, and swung as hard as he could.

The flat of the shovel struck Rebecca square in the face, shattering her nose and sending her eyes rolling back. In what seemed like slow motion, Rebecca fell in an arc to the floor and went quiet.

Everyone held still, waiting for her to suddenly lunge up like killers always seemed to.

But she didn't.

Satisfied that she was unconscious, Joe stepped over and helped Zachary to his feet.

It wasn't easy for Zachary, but he made it. Shakily.

Sam got to her feet, too, and, though winded, was smiling.

"Hear that?" she said, gesturing outside.

The sound was faint, but there was no mistaking it: sirens.

"We better get outside so they can find us," Joe said.

Zachary grinned. For once, Joe wanted the police to find him.

Sam was beside him, then, putting an arm around his middle. He flinched.

"C'mon, tough guy," she said. "You've taken enough abuse for one day. Be a man and take some help, huh?"

And that was fine by him. So he leaned on her, and together the three of them made it outside.

36

The pain upon waking encompassed all. Gone were the memories, the shame. Gone, the facade.

Now there was only the pain.

And the hate for those who had caused it.

She rolled over and pushed up to her hands and knees. The pain in her face was eye-watering. But she remembered how to use it. How to change it into strength. How to channel all that distilled hatred into the fibers of her muscles, enlivening her.

Breathing was especially difficult, but she managed, hot, coppery gasps that hissed from behind her clenched teeth.

Wincing, she stood and went through the garage door where that homeless bum had sneaked in. Through the dark, she went out the side door into the bright daylight once again.

They had left her there and they had moved on. She could hear them around the front of the house. Them, and the sirens, close now. Still, there was time. There had to be time.

She moved carefully toward the fence in the backyard,

and then toward the gate, peering through the spaces in the warped wood until she could see them.

The ones that had tried to escape her. They seemed so at ease. They didn't know. And that made her want to laugh. She didn't, though. She would laugh as she squeezed the life out of the last of them. Oh, how she would laugh.

And then the moment presented itself to her, so perfect, as the police car pulled up on the opposite side of the street. Its lights were flashing, and that hurt her eyes, but she saw Sam run over to talk to the officer. The old bum was behind her, hesitant but still trying to be helpful.

And Zachary? They'd left Zachary sitting on the empty flower box at the edge of the front patio.

She would move now, knowing that this would be her last act on this godforsaken earth.

She was ready. She deserved the rest. As for the others? Let them watch. Even this close, they could not stop her. She would make Zachary bleed and that would make them bleed, too.

37

Zachary watched as Sam and Joe explained what was going on to the police. Only one car had arrived, but it sounded like more were in the distance.

Probably an ambulance, too.

At least Zachary hoped so. He wasn't keen to voice it aloud, but he was more than a little concerned about his injuries. He was especially having a tough time catching his breath and he wondered if maybe that meant he'd broken a rib.

He inhaled as deeply as he comfortably could, feeling a bit woozy, and then let the breath out, paying careful attention to the areas that hurt him.

Then, when he had no breath left in him, something wrapped around his throat from behind and he found that he couldn't breathe at all.

He tilted his head back and there she was again, suddenly in his vision, smiling horribly through bloody teeth.

Rebecca.

He couldn't cry out. He couldn't breathe.

Her hands closed more tightly around his neck, and she pulled him backwards off the planter onto the patio. She was sitting down now, he realized, using her legs to pin his arms to the ground.

Spots danced before his eyes.

He didn't know how long he had before everything went black, but he knew it wasn't long.

Seconds? If he was lucky.

He tried to fight, willed himself to fight. To do something. Anything.

It was hard, though.

It would be easier to let go.

To float away into the black.

Then the thought came to him with a primordial strength.

NO.

The force of what may have been the first word, the first primitive assertion.

NO.

And he could not see but he knew Rebecca's face, had dreamed of it in better days, knew it as well as his own.

The strength of that primitive assertion of survival took that knowledge and used it.

He put his feet on the planter and pushed himself backward as hard as he could. His head pressed into her breasts and then she went over. Her legs went up and Zachary pulled his arms free and found her eyes with his thumbs. And though she screamed and struggled to get away, his hands had found her hair. He held her and he squeezed until his hands were wet. She let go then and air flooded into his lungs. A brilliant light came with it, pushing the darkness out of his vision and dizzying him.

Suddenly, the world rushed in, so much movement and sound, total chaos.

And Sam was beside him, then, sobbing. Joe looked like he was going to throw up.

An ambulance came, and the paramedics were trying to convince Sam that it would be okay to leave his side. He squeezed her hand and gave her a small nod, and she kissed his forehead.

The police—there were more of them now—were standing over Rebecca's body. And now he knew why Joe looked sick. Her face wasn't there anymore. It was just black holes in a mask of red. Zachary turned away quickly. He felt sick, too.

As they loaded him in the ambulance, he heard one of the paramedics arguing outside. Then he heard one voice above the others: "I'm riding with him because I'm his girlfriend, asshole."

He lifted his head and saw Sam, beautiful Sam, climbing into the back with him.

She took his hands in hers and said, "We're going to be okay now. We're okay."

And she kissed him softly.

But she was wrong.

They had lived through hell. The way he figured it, things could only get better from here.

They were going to be better than okay.